Her mother was replacing her.

Christina propped her arms on the track railing, watching her mother canter Star around the oval. It was early Wednesday morning, the second time Ashleigh had ridden Star. The colt's chestnut coat gleamed, and his thick tail streamed behind him.

Leaning slightly forward in the saddle, Ashleigh swayed rhythmically with the colt's stride. The two moved so smoothly, they seemed to float. Her mother's cheeks were flushed, and when Star breezed past, an elated smile lit up Ashleigh's face.

They went great together.

Christina bit back her feelings of jealousy. Her mother had scrapbooks filled with articles and mementos about Wonder and all her wins. Christina had wanted her own scrapbook filled with stories about Star. But now her mother was replacing her.

THOROUGHBRED

LIVING LEGEND

CREATED BY
JOANNA CAMPBELL

WRITTEN BY
ALICE LEONHARDT

HarperEntertainment
An Imprint of HarperCollins*Publishers*

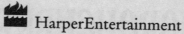

HarperEntertainment

An Imprint of HarperCollins*Publishers*
10 East 53rd Street, New York, NY 10022-5299

Copyright © 2000 by 17th Street Productions, Inc. and Joanna Campbell

 Produced by 17th Street Productions, a division of Daniel Weiss Associates, Inc.

HarperCollins books are available at special quantity discounts for bulk purchases for sales promotions, premiums, or fund-raising. For information, please call or write: Special Markets Department, HarperCollins Publishers, 10 East 53rd Street, New York, NY 10022-5299. Telephone: (212) 207-7528. Fax: (212) 207-7222.

ISBN 0-06-106633-8

HarperCollins®, ■®, and HarperEntertainment™ are trademarks of HarperCollins Publishers Inc.

Cover art © 1999 by Daniel Weiss Associates, Inc.

First printing: February 2000

Printed in the United States of America

Visit HarperEntertainment on the World Wide Web at
www.harpercollins.com

❖ 10 9 8 7 6 5 4 3 2

LIVING
LEGEND

1

CHRISTINA REESE DROPPED THE BRUSH IN THE AISLE FOR THE third time that morning. When she picked it up, Wonder's Star, the big chestnut Thoroughbred who was hooked to crossties, turned his head to stare at her with curious brown eyes.

"All right. I'm clumsy, I know," Christina told the two-year-old colt as she finished brushing his silky neck. "I can't help it. I'm too nervous."

Star bobbed his head, the crossties jingling, as if he agreed with Christina. Except for one of the barn hands mucking stalls, the two were alone in the training barn at Whitebrook Farm, the Thoroughbred farm where Christina lived. The rest of the grooms and exercise riders had taken the other colts and fillies in training down to the practice track for their early morning workouts.

Christina was stalling.

"It's just that after your win in the Kentucky Stakes, everybody's going to be watching us," Christina explained to Star. "We can't make any mistakes."

It was Tuesday, and Brad and Lavinia Townsend had come to watch the colt's last workout at Whitebrook before Star's race on Saturday at Churchill Downs. The Townsends shared ownership of Star with Christina's mother and father, Ashleigh Griffen and Mike Reese. Christina and Star had won their first race two weeks earlier, but Brad and Lavinia still made her nervous. No matter how fast Star breezed, they always found fault with something.

"Well, I'd better tack you up before they wonder where we are." With a sigh, Christina dropped the brush in the grooming box.

A voice rang down the aisle. "Hey, Chris, did you fall asleep in here?" Christina's cousin, Melanie Graham, came striding into the barn carrying a newspaper. "They're getting restless down there. Lavinia wanted to come in after you, but I told her I'd go and get you."

"Thanks for saving me." Christina hurried into the tack room to get a bridle and saddle. When she came out, Melanie was standing at Star's head, holding up the front page of the sports section of the newspaper. Christina halted and read the headline out loud. "'Will Wonder's Wonderful Colt Win the Spring Stakes?'"

2

"It's from this morning's paper," Melanie said, tapping the page. "It's all about you and Star and your mom and Wonder. I thought the headline was pretty clever. I'll save the article for you so you can add it to your scrapbook, okay?"

"Thanks." Christina had been flattered by all the publicity after Star's win. Already she had six articles in the scrapbook she'd started—a record of her and Star's racing career.

"Gee, I wish the newspaper wrote all those nice things about *me*," Melanie teased, although Christina knew her cousin wasn't really jealous. Melanie already had five wins under her belt, and she was a fearless "bug"—the common term for an apprentice jockey.

Christina rolled her eyes as she put the pad and saddle on Star's back. "You know the paper's making a big deal out of Star only because of Mom and Wonder." Ashleigh and Wonder had won the Kentucky Derby, among many other prestigious races. "I can't believe all this hype. I mean, Star and I won only one race," she scoffed. "It's like they've forgotten all about Star's *first* race, which was pretty memorable for how slow he went."

"But that's because you weren't riding him," Melanie pointed out as she took the bridle from Christina.

"True." Naomi Traeger, another jockey who often rode for Whitebrook, had ridden Star in his first race, and he'd been slow as a turtle.

About a month earlier, Christina had passed her test to become an apprentice jockey. Since the stewards had given her only conditional approval, they were going to review her next two races. She'd ridden Star in the Kentucky Stakes and won, which counted for one race. She'd have to prove herself this Saturday before she could be confident that she had her apprentice license for sure.

Melanie unhooked the crossties and began to bridle Star. "This guy will run his heart out for you, so don't let the Townsends psych you out."

"You're right. It's just that with all that's happened . . ." Christina's voice trailed off as she thought back to a year before, when Star was being trained at Townsend Acres. She'd had a terrible time convincing Brad that his training methods were only making Star fearful and aggressive. Luckily, her parents had finally seen her side of things and decided to bring Star back to Whitebrook.

But Brad still had the last word. He'd strongly opposed having Christina jockey Star in the Kentucky Stakes, since it was her first race. Melanie had been scheduled to ride the colt, but at the last minute she faked a sprained wrist so Christina could ride him instead. If they had lost, Christina knew, Brad would have been furious enough to insist that Star go back to Townsend Acres.

The thought made Christina shudder. That was the *last* thing she wanted. Ever since Wonder—Star's dam— had died and Christina had nursed the little orphaned colt, she had felt a special bond with Star. In the past year, as they trained for and won their first race together, their bond had grown even stronger.

Christina was so committed to Star that she had sold her eventing horse, Sterling Dream, to Tor and Samantha Nelson, her former trainers. Samantha had leased Sterling to Kaitlin Boyce, who was sixteen, too, and as horse-crazy as Christina. The Nelsons' farm, Whisperwood, was just down the road, so Christina could still visit the mare whenever she wanted.

"Star's ready," Melanie said, handing the reins to Christina. "Go out there and strut your stuff."

Christina laughed. "What would I do without you, Mel?"

"Sometimes I wonder." When Melanie had arrived from New York City three years earlier, the two cousins had been anything but close. But their love of horses had brought them together, and now they were best friends.

"Kevin's waiting on old Thunder," Melanie added. "Mike wants him to breeze with you to give you a little competition."

"Any other surprises?" Putting on her helmet,

Christina tucked her strawberry blond hair underneath.

Melanie grinned mischievously. "Parker's here, too."

"Oh, *great*." Christina had been dating Parker Townsend, Brad and Lavinia's son, for the past year. It wasn't that she minded him watching her ride—they'd ridden together hundreds of times—but it just added to the pressure.

"And one more thing," Melanie said as Christina led Star outside. "Your parents have turned this into a little party to celebrate the new Star. Everyone's invited to brunch afterward."

Christina groaned. "But he's not a star yet!"

"According to Brad, he's the next Derby winner," Melanie said, laughing.

"Talk about high expectations," Christina grumbled.

"Quit worrying." Melanie gave her a leg up. "You're going to leave Kevin in the dust."

Christina hoped Melanie was right. She turned Star around, walking him across the grassy area between Whitebrook's three barns. The colt's stride was long and loose, and his ears were pricked as he gazed at the early morning hustle and bustle typical of a busy training and breeding farm.

Christina knew Star had what it took to be a champion, but he was only two years old, and she didn't want to rush him. In the Kentucky Stakes Star had come from dead last to beat the other horses. This Saturday he'd have to prove that he could win again.

Naomi was riding Fast Gun, a fractious four-year-old, down the path from the training track. Ashleigh and Mike were training the colt for Kimberley McFarland, one of their new clients. Raising her whip in the air, Naomi waved at Christina, then turned her attention back to her mount. Naomi was twenty and had been working at Whitebrook for years. Now she was a full-fledged jockey, but she still came to the farm to work horses during the week.

"How'd he do?" Christina asked as the colt jigged past, his bay coat dark with sweat. The rising sun was already hot, the morning sky hazy.

"He was a handful," Naomi admitted. Her long braid flopped against her back as Fast Gun lunged at Star, who only cocked his ears curiously. Christina laughed. She knew there was only one thing on Star's mind that morning—his work. Not only had he inherited his dam's speed, he had her intelligence, too.

"But he sure is fast. We'll see how he does Saturday." Naomi turned Fast Gun in a circle, trying to keep him from running off.

As Christina rode Star to the track, she spotted Lavinia and Brad standing by the rail talking to Mike and Ashleigh. Even at eight in the morning, the

Townsends looked as if they were going to a cocktail party. Lavinia wore a figure-hugging linen sheath, heels, and a wide-brimmed hat. Brad wore a navy sport coat and khakis. In contrast, Christina's mom and dad wore barn clothes—jeans, polo shirts, and paddock boots. It was easy to see who spent hands-on time with the horses.

Brad had a stopwatch hanging on a cord around his neck. As Christina passed the group she waved hello, then rode Star through the gap and onto the track.

Gazing around, Christina hunted for Parker. He was perched on the track's top rail talking to Kevin McLean, who was mounted on Thunder, a retired racehorse they used for training the younger Thoroughbreds. Kevin was the son of Ian McLean, Whitebrook's head trainer, and he and Christina had grown up together. Even though he'd grown too tall to be a jockey, Kevin was a gifted rider who loved to win—at any sport. Christina knew that he'd give her plenty of competition that morning.

"Good luck," Parker called, his blue eyes smiling under the brim of his baseball cap. Parker was tall and lanky, and he looked so cute draped over the top fence board in a worn white T-shirt and faded blue jeans that Christina couldn't help but smile happily.

"You're supposed to be wishing *me* good luck," Kevin told Parker before steering Thunder alongside Star. "Ready to lose, Chris?"

"In your dreams," Christina said. She and Kevin were always teasing each other. "I'm going to leave you two in the dust!"

Squeezing her heels against Star's sides, she urged him into a trot to warm up. Perched high, her stirrups short, Christina posted to his long stride. Behind her, she could hear Thunder canter to catch up. When they approached the starting gate, Christina saw Ian and Maureen Mack, his assistant trainer, waiting to help them load. Star arched his neck and pranced excitedly.

"You're ready to race, aren't you?" Christina said, patting his neck. She balanced her weight between her knees and feet, hovering over the pommel, moving easily with Star's stride. Part of the jockey's job was to keep the horse calm and focused until the beginning of the race. Christina always felt a little nervous when they loaded into the two-and-a-half-foot-wide gate and the door was shut behind them. To earn her apprentice certificate, she'd had to practice breaking from the gate hundreds of times, and Whitebrook Farm took extra care to teach their youngsters to load and break safely. Still, in the pre-race excitement and confusion, many horses forgot their early training and acted up.

She slowed Star to a walk. "Good luck," Maureen called as she opened the door to the gate. Star walked in calmly, but Christina could feel the tenseness in his muscles, and when the metal door slammed behind them, they both jumped anxiously.

Kevin walked Thunder into the gate next to them. "Did I tell you about the horse that flipped over in one of these?" he whispered, just loud enough for Christina to hear.

Ignoring him, Christina clenched her jaw. She knew Kevin was trying to distract her. Crouching low over Star's neck, she wrapped a small hunk of mane around her fingers. All her attention was on the task ahead.

Ian would sound the starter's gun. When Star broke from the gate, she needed to be right with him. Races could be won or lost at the starting gate.

"Ready?" Ian called from the sidelines.

Christina nodded. Sweat dripped from under her helmet. Star pranced in place, and she scratched his neck with one finger. "Almost. Almost," she crooned. "Steady—"

The gun went off.

"Go!" Christina whispered urgently as the front door banged open and Star leaped from the gate. Thunder broke at the same instant.

Stride for stride the two horses blew down the track. Hunched over Star's neck, eyes forward, Christina sat quietly. Her hands were firm on the reins, her fingers taking and giving as she communicated to Star.

She could feel his powerful muscles move underneath her as his long stride ate up the track. If she let him go, Star would run as hard and as fast as he could. She had to keep him rated so he wouldn't tire and would have enough to make a move at the last furlong.

Christina glanced sideways. Kevin was already ahead by half a length. He was crouched over Thunder, his arms pumping, his body rocking. Thunder looked like he was giving it all he had.

Christina bent a little lower, relaxed her elbows, and let her fingers grow softer on the reins. "Now," she whispered.

In response, Star flattened his ears. Then his stride lengthened and Christina could feel his speed increase dramatically, as if he'd shifted gears. Effortlessly Star streaked past Thunder and pounded down the backstretch, reaching the wire two lengths ahead. He could have galloped on, but Christina stood in her stirrups, signaling him to slow. A triumphant smile spread across her face when she head her father shout, "A black-letter workout!" Brad and Lavinia clapped politely.

The best work time over a specific distance on a given day at each track was printed in the racing dailies—thus the term black-letter workout. It was Christina and Star's first one.

Even before her father shouted out their time Christina knew by the way Star felt that it had been their fastest work yet. The colt would have no problem winning on Saturday. He was a true champion—getting faster and braver the more he raced.

"A toast all around." Brad Townsend raised his glass. Smiling, Christina raised her soda glass along with the crowd packed in the Reeses' family room for brunch.

"To Wonder's Star, the next Kentucky Derby winner," Brad said, his voice booming. "Like his dam, Wonder, he'll make Townsend Acres and Whitebrook Farm proud."

As Christina clinked glasses with her mother, she noted the excited expressions on her parents' and the Townsends' faces. They began to chatter enthusiastically about Star's times and which races he would run in the next year. Christina couldn't believe how well the four were getting along.

All because of Star, Christina thought. And it was a good thing. So why did her stomach feel so queasy?

Maybe she was hungry. Setting down her glass, she went into the kitchen. Maureen, Ian, and several of the farm's grooms were standing by the sink, talking about the upcoming race. Kevin, Parker, and Melanie were hanging around the table, where a buffet of food was laid out. As Christina reached for a paper plate she heard them arguing.

"Don't you think I should put some money on Star

this weekend?" Kevin asked Christina. "Melanie says it's too risky. But I say he's a sure win. And I could sure use the money for new basketball shoes."

"W-Well, I . . . ," Christina stammered. Suddenly her stomach rolled. "Excuse me," she croaked. "I think I need some fresh air." Dropping the plate, she hurried into the laundry room. She could hear Parker call her name, but she didn't stop. Grabbing a light jacket, she ran out the door.

She needed to get away from the party. She needed to see Star.

Breaking into a jog, she crossed the yard and hurried up the drive, which was illuminated by the outdoor lights. When she reached Star's stall, she flung open the door. Startled, he stared at her with huge eyes. A hunk of the hay he was having for dinner hung from his mouth.

"Hey, handsome." Christina flung her arms around the colt's neck. Star resumed crunching, and as she listened to the rhythmic clunk of his jaws, the knots in her stomach loosened.

"Chris?"

Christina swung around to see Parker standing in the open doorway.

"Hiding out?" he asked as he stepped inside. Star stopped chewing to stare at him.

"How'd you guess?"

Parker grinned. "Because I know you." Taking a step closer, he reached out and flicked a piece of hay from Christina's shirt collar, his eyes never leaving hers. "I know how anxious you were before the last race. And now with everyone making such a big deal out of the race on Saturday, you've got to be more than a little worried. Am I right?"

"Boy, are you ever." A sudden flash of anxiety made Christina turn away. "I'm afraid we can't live up to everybody's expectations," she said. Putting her hand on Star's neck, she ruffled his soft mane.

"Hey, if Star runs like he did this morning, you'll win, no problem."

"I know Star's fast. He could have run forever this morning, but your parents—"

"Are bossy and pushy and rude?" Parker joked.

Christina giggled. Even though Parker had made the decision to stay home at Townsend Acres and work things out with his parents, he still didn't get along with them very well.

"All they want is for Star to win, win, win. He's only two. I don't want him to burn out or, even worse, break a leg!" The thought brought tears to Christina's eyes.

"Hey." Parker put a hand on her shoulder. "No one wants Star to break down. Especially not my dad. And your parents are pacing his races carefully. All of them want Star to do well."

Christina smiled, feeling a little better. "It is pretty amazing," she said, her thoughts going back to the party. "Your parents and mine getting along—it's like Star's win has brought the two farms together. But what if he loses?"

"Don't think about that. You're going to do great on Saturday," Parker told her. He wrapped his arm around Christina's shoulders. "And even if you don't," he added, his eyes twinkling, "you'll still be the cutest jockey in Kentucky."

"Would you be serious?" Christina pushed him away. "Listen, I need to tell you something. It's about the Kentucky Stakes."

"You cheated!" Parker looked down at her, his eyes wide with pretend horror.

"Worse. After the race all those people and reporters were asking how it felt to win. I was so pumped up, I felt really confident. But when the excitement died down, I started thinking about that race, and I realized we only won because of Star. I actually did a terrible job!"

Parker laughed. "You didn't do a terrible job. Okay, so you were dead last until the last furlong. But you steered Star around a whole field of horses and you won. Plus it was only your first race. Just think how well the two of you will do when you have more experience."

"You think?"

"I think." Parker grinned down at her.

Star pushed his nose into her hand and snorted noisily. Christina put her arms around the colt's neck and gave him a good night hug.

"I hope you're right, Parker," she said. "I really do."

2

WHEN CHRISTINA PULLED THE BLUE-AND-WHITE SILK JERSEY
over her head, a thrill of excitement tingled through her.
She and Melanie were changing in the women's locker
room at Churchill Downs. It was late Saturday morning. In an hour she would be racing Star in the Spring
Stakes.

Melanie was riding in two other races. For now she
wore a red-and-white jersey, the colors of Rushing
Creek Farm. She was riding an old friend of hers, Heart
of Stone, for his owners, Jeff and Sarilee Owens, in the
third race. Stoney had been bred and trained at Whitebrook. This spring Melanie had already ridden him to
two wins.

After Stoney's race Melanie would change silks and
ride Wind Chaser in the fifth race for Ian McLean and

Sam. Father and daughter had invested their savings in the talented Thoroughbred, and it had certainly paid off. Wind Chaser had won all but two of his starts and had brought in a lot of purse money. Naomi had been his first jockey, but as Melanie became more experienced, she'd started riding him.

"If I win both races today," Melanie chattered as she pulled on her lightweight black boots, "I'll be that much closer to being a real jockey."

"Then what? Do you think you'll get an agent and go professional?" Christina asked, her mind not really on the conversation. She was thinking about Star's workout on Thursday at the Churchill Downs track. Even the official clocker had been impressed. Star had barely broken a sweat, but their time had still been record fast.

"That's the plan," Melanie said as she smoothed a red-and-white cover on her helmet. "Just don't tell my dad. He'll go ballistic. He thinks that when I graduate next year I'm coming back to New York and going to college."

"College?" Christina choked down a bubble of laughter. Melanie's grades had never been very good. She studied just hard enough to keep from getting F's for fear that Will Graham, her father, would ground her from riding. Will and his wife, Susan, were record producers who lived in New York City. They allowed

18

Melanie to live in Kentucky so she could stay out of trouble and be near the horses that she loved so much.

"Does he know how into racing you are?" Christina asked.

"Not really. In our phone conversations I talk about everything *but* racing. I mean, he knows I'm an apprentice jockey, but I don't think he realizes I'm exercise-riding every day and racing every weekend."

Christina shook her head. She couldn't imagine having the kind of long-distance relationship with her dad that Melanie had with Will, though it seemed to work for them. "When's he coming to watch a race?"

Melanie grimaced. "I hope never. That way he'll never know how dangerous it is. Ready? We can watch films from the last races while we wait."

"Ugh." Christina remembered watching the film from the Kentucky Stakes with the other bugs the Monday after the race. She'd been embarrassed to see what a lousy job she'd done. That was how she knew that if it hadn't been for Star's power and speed, there was no way they could have won.

"Maybe I can see my win on Pride's Heart last Sunday," Melanie said as she tucked her jersey into her nylon pants.

"Sounding a little conceited, aren't we?" Christina joked.

"Well, I did *win*," Melanie replied, grinning. "And

all the other jockeys get so mad when a bug beats them. I like to rub it in whenever I can."

Carrying her lightweight racing saddle, Christina followed Melanie into the main area of the jockey room. It was a big room equipped with a kitchen, two TVs, and a pool table. Doors led to the men's locker room, the sauna, and a massage room.

About twenty other jockeys were getting ready for the day's races. Some were sprawled in chairs watching the previous week's race replays or talking. Many of the top jockeys had valets who took care of their equipment and helped them stay organized from one race to the next.

Christina had already weighed in with the clerk of scales. Since she was a bug and riding a two-year-old, she was allowed a low weight. Fortunately, she'd had no problems staying under 110 pounds. Some of the bigger jockeys, however, had to sweat it out in the hot box or fast for a day before they got on the scale.

"Hey, here come some *bugs*," one of the jockeys relaxing in a chair said. "Anybody got a flyswatter?" Christina recognized Raoul, one of the older jockeys. No one knew exactly how old he was, but rumor had it he'd been racing for half a century.

"I've got some bug spray," another jockey chimed in. Sammy Fingers—at least that was what everyone called him since a horse had bitten off one of his fingers. "Label says it works on flies, fleas, ticks—even stinkbugs," Sammy added, waving an imaginary can around the room.

"Then you'd better use it on yourself," Melanie shot back as she pulled a chair up in front of the TV screen. She sniffed the air. "'Cause you sure do smell. What kind of cologne is that? Eau de manure?"

Everybody cracked up. Christina forced a smile. The jockeys always teased each other—it was part of the game. Most of the banter was harmless, but often the joking covered up real gripes. Melanie got right into it, but Christina felt the underlying tension, and it made her uneasy.

Many of the journeymen—as the professionals were called—thought it unfair that apprentice jockeys rode with lighter weights. In addition, they accused the inexperienced bugs of reckless riding and causing accidents. Since all jockeys got a percentage of the purse money, they were out to win. Most were fiercely competitive—on and off the track.

"Those bugs had better watch themselves today," a dark-haired jockey named George said, his voice just loud enough for Melanie and Christina to hear. "They're getting too cocky for their own good."

"Jealous, George?" Melanie asked. George was leaning against the wall, a scowl on his face. Christina noticed he was wearing black and red silks—Townsend Acres' colors.

The jockey uncrossed his arms. "No way. You young kids think you know everything—but you don't have a clue. That's why you should stay off the track." Glaring at Melanie, he strode from the room.

"Don't pay any attention to him," said Vicky Frontiere, a jockey friend of Ashleigh's. She walked over to the two girls. For the past few years Vicky had been riding on the West Coast. This spring she'd moved to the Kentucky tracks and had helped Christina test for her jockey license. "He's just mad 'cause he's not riding as many horses as he used to."

"Why not?" Christina asked.

"He hasn't been winning enough, so trainers don't want to use him. He used to ride all the big-time stakes horses. Now his agent can only get him on claimers."

"I can see why," Melanie said. "He's mean."

Vicky shrugged. "Yeah, but you've got to remember this is his job. If he doesn't ride, he doesn't get paid. He's got a family to support." She took a sip from the bottle of water in her hand.

"Townsend Acres is obviously still using him," Melanie mentioned. "He's riding one of their two-year-olds, Hail to Victory, in the first race."

Christina arched an eyebrow. Brad was racing one of his colts against Star? *Well, Star isn't a Townsend Acres horse, anyway*, she reminded herself.

Over the speaker system, Christina heard the track announcer welcome the crowd to Churchill Downs. She stood and picked up her saddle.

"Good luck, Chris." Melanie gave her a thumbs-up sign. "I'll be watching." George, Sammy Fingers, another bug named Ronnie, and three jockeys Christina didn't recognize walked out with her. On the way out, George and Sammy pushed right in front of Christina, deliberately knocking her into the doorjamb.

"Oh, excuse us," George said with mock politeness. "We didn't see you. Kind of like the way these bugs ride right into you on the track, isn't it, Sammy?"

Sammy chuckled. "Yeah, us old jocks have to look out for ourselves." He shot Christina such a cold look, it gave her goose bumps. "Watch out, *bug*," he added, his tone ominous. Laughing, George pretended to pump a can of spray in the air, and when the two left, they let the door close in her face.

Christina blew out a shaky breath. As she followed them to the paddock, her stomach churned. *They're just taunting you,* she told herself. *They don't mean anything by it.*

Or did they?

Not only did George have a chip on his shoulder, he was riding for Brad. Had Brad told him to give her a hard time?

Christina shook the thought from her mind. She

23

couldn't let her fears of losing get to her. No matter what happened, she had to ride a great race.

As soon as Christina reached the paddock and saw Star, she forgot her worries. He looked so handsome striding next to Mike, his coppery coat glistening in the sun, his neck arched and his eyes bright and alert.

Quickly Christina appraised the other two-year-olds entered in the six-and-a-half-furlong race. She spotted Ralph Dunkirk leading Hail to Victory, Townsend Acres' leggy gray. He was rangy and powerful-looking, but Star was a better class of horse. And she wasn't the only one who thought so. She could hear several onlookers murmur Star's name as she walked by.

Star had drawn the number four gate position, so Christina followed Mike and Star into the fourth saddling stall. "He passed the vet check with flying colors," Mike said. He took the saddle from her, giving Christina a chance to greet Star and press a kiss on his velvety muzzle.

"I'm glad *you're* calm," she murmured to the colt as he blew softly against her cheek. "Because I'm not!"

"How are you doing?" her father asked as he smoothed the blanket with the number four on Star's back before putting on the tiny racing saddle.

Christina smiled. "Great!" she chirped, too enthusiastically. Her father gave her an odd look before going around Star's rump to the right side.

Christina grabbed the girth her father passed under the colt's belly.

"Chris," he said when he came back around to her side, "there's nothing wrong with feeling nervous. *I'm* nervous and I'm not even riding. And your mother's so nervous, she stayed on the backside with Wind Chaser. But don't worry—at post time she'll be right at the rail watching your every move."

Just what I need, Christina thought, chewing her lip. Should she tell her dad about George's comments? No. Her father would just tell her what she already knew—all jockeys were out to win. She had to learn to be thick-skinned, like Melanie.

"I just want to be the best jockey for Star," Christina said, tightening the colt's girth.

Her father gave her shoulders a squeeze. "You *are* the best jockey. Star told me."

"Oh, Dad." Christina rolled her eyes.

"He did! As soon as he saw you come into the paddock, he nickered, 'There's my favorite jockey!' I heard him clearly. You were just too worried to notice. And if it's worth anything"—he grinned—"you're *my* favorite jockey, too."

Christina hugged her dad. "You're just saying that because I'm your daughter. I know Brad wishes a more experienced jockey were riding Star."

"Riders up!" the paddock judge called out.

Mike led Star from the stall, then gave Christina a leg up. Once she was in the saddle with the reins in her hands, Christina felt a little of her confidence return. This was where she belonged.

"Who should I watch out for?" she asked her father.

He nodded toward the gray. "Brad's colt is fast and will probably set the pace. So is number three, Turnabout, though he's a wild man until the gates open. Also, Jeremy Rush is on Hornet's Nest and he's in the number one spot. He's a really experienced jockey. He'll probably break fast and get the best position."

"Sounds like a tough race," Christina murmured, "against some tough jocks."

Her father glanced up at her as he led her to the paddock gate. "You're a winning jock, Chris, and don't you forget it."

She grinned. "Thanks, Dad. Any other instructions?"

"Just listen to your horse. He'll tell you what to do."

"We're counting on you, Christina!" another voice boomed from the sidelines. Christina snapped her head around. Brad stood alongside the paddock gate. Lavinia was beside him wearing a sleeveless red silk blouse and black skirt—the Townsend colors. When she waved at Christina, her wrist glittered with gold jewelry.

26

Are you sure you want me to win? Christina wanted to retort, but she smiled politely instead. At the gate Mike patted her knee reassuringly. "Don't pay attention to them. Focus on the race."

Then Christina saw her mother push through the crowd and up to the paddock gate. "Good luck," Ashleigh called, a smile of pride on her face.

Christina gave her mother a thumbs-up sign, then followed Sammy Fingers on the number three horse, Turnabout, out onto the track for the post parade. He was a rangy bay with a wild eye, and he fought against the pony horse with every step. Christina glanced behind her at George, on Hail to Victory. George touched the handle of his whip to his helmet as if to salute her, but his grin was menacing.

Christina swung back around and gathered up her reins. She needed to forget Sammy and George and concentrate on Star. Although most of the Thoroughbreds were escorted by pony horses, Christina had chosen to ride to the gate without one.

As they walked past the packed grandstand Christina kept her eyes straight ahead. "We'll show them," she whispered to Star. She scratched his withers. "This time we have to break clean and stay with the field. No crazy running from last place."

As if heeding her words, Star bobbed his head and broke into a relaxed canter. Christina stood in the saddle, letting him move under her as they warmed up. Then it was time to walk to the starting gate. Christina circled Star while the gate handlers loaded the horses. Sammy's horse, number three, reared and ran backward. Linking hands, two handlers got behind him, pushed him into the gate, then slammed it shut.

Christina was next.

Star walked in calmly, but Christina could feel the tenseness in his powerful muscles. He was coiled like a spring, ready for the moment of takeoff.

Christina took a deep breath, adjusted her goggles, and perched low over Star's neck. She wound a hunk of mane around one gloved finger.

Beside her, Sammy's horse reared, then hit the wall with a bang, making Star jump. The assistant starter, propped on a small ledge on the gate wall, reached up to grab the cheekpiece of Star's bridle.

"That's okay," Christina told him. "Star's cool."

"Hey, bug," she heard George hiss on her other side, "watch out."

"You're the one who needs to watch out, George!" Christina snapped, the tension getting to her.

The assistant starter laughed, and George snorted under his breath.

"One back!" Christina heard the handlers cry. Ducking her head, she wiped her sweaty temples with her wrist. One more horse to load.

Christina took a firm hold on the reins and swallowed the lump that clogged her throat. *We can do it,* she said silently.

"It's post time!" the announcer called across the track. Then the starter's gun went off, a bell rang, and the front doors banged open.

"They're off!"

3

Star shot from the starting gate so fast, Christina was jerked backward. Luckily, she kept her grip on his mane and quickly rebalanced herself. Ahead, the track stretched like a smooth landing strip. No one was in front of her. She was in first place! Peering sideways, she saw the field of horses galloping in a jagged line across the width of the track.

Then Christina realized Star was beginning to run out of control. His head was stretched low and his stride was long and ragged. She had to get him rated or he'd burn himself out.

"Easy," she crooned as she tugged on the reins with her fingers. Star cocked one ear, listening, and short-ened his stride ever so slightly. Beside them, two horses forged ahead, while two horses on the outside

30

started to swerve toward the inside rail.

For a moment Christina panicked as the field of horses thundered all around her. The pounding of hooves was deafening. Dirt flew in the air, whacking her goggles and cheeks. Ahead of her, the jockeys on the number six and seven horses hollered at each other.

Christina checked the post as they galloped past. Second furlong. They had a little over four to go. She needed to move Star into a better position. This time she was determined not to get stuck in the back of the field.

"Hornet's Nest is on the rail. Turnabout and Hail to Victory are fighting for second place. Wonder's Star is running a strong fourth with Caliber closing," the announcer's voice rang out.

Christina blocked out the sound. She didn't want to have to rely on the announcer to tell her who was in the lead.

In front of her, Hail to Victory and Turnabout ran neck and neck. Hornet's Nest hugged the rail. The rest of the field was behind her. As they approached the fourth pole Christina thought she was in a good spot. When one of the other colts started lagging, she'd find an opening and urge Star through. She could feel the strength in his stride. His nostrils weren't even flared. As soon as she gave the signal, he'd be ready to kick it into high gear.

As they came around the final turn Hail to Victory

swung wide toward the outside. Christina saw her spot. "Go," she whispered to Star, and flattened her body against the crest of his neck.

The colt's front legs seemed to reach out and grab the surface of the track as he flew between the two horses. Then Hail to Victory suddenly cut back toward Turnabout. George dropped his whip hand and in one quick move whacked Star on his nose.

Startled, the colt bobbled. Hail to Victory and Turnabout closed up the hole. Christina was boxed in again. She'd have to go around!

But it was too late. Christina could feel Star hesitate, responding to her own indecision. His ears flicked back as he waited for her signal. Christina knew that if she drove him around the others, he'd try with all his heart to win. But at what price?

The quarter pole flashed by. Christina made her decision. She wouldn't risk injuring Star in order to win. Holding her fourth-place position, Christina and Star galloped toward the finish line.

"And it's Hornet's Nest by a length, followed by Hail to Victory and Turnabout," the announcer hollered as the horses charged over the finish line. "Wonder's Star, the winner of the Kentucky Stakes three weeks ago, is a disappointing fourth."

Disappointing is right, Christina thought as she stood in her stirrups. Ahead of her, Christina saw Sammy and

George trot their horses close enough to slap palms.

She knew they'd boxed her in on purpose; one of them had even sacrificed a win to make sure she lost. She could protest, but she doubted it would do any good. George and Sammy had been careful that their moves didn't look deliberate, and the camera probably hadn't picked up George's left side—his whip side—so the officials wouldn't be able to see how he'd hit Star. If Christina protested, she'd be branded as a sore loser and a troublemaker.

Christina had to face it. She'd been outmaneuvered by two experienced jockeys.

Leaning back, Christina asked Star to slow to a trot. Jerking the reins through her fingers, he lowered his head and gave it an impatient shake. Christina knew what he was trying to tell her. He wanted to keep running.

Christina sighed. "Sorry, big guy. I blew it. A better jockey wouldn't have gotten trapped like that." She slowed Star to a bouncy walk. As they headed down the track Ashleigh came through the gate to meet them, her brows raised in a question. Christina didn't know what to tell her.

Christina gulped. Her mother would definitely be disappointed that her daughter was obviously *not* following in her footsteps.

Christina halted Star, and Ashleigh snapped a lead

line to his bridle. "What happened out there, Chris?" she asked, her face showing worry.

"I got boxed in. I'm sorry," Christina apologized as she slid off the colt's back, landing hard in the dirt. "He was running strong, and if we'd had another few furlongs, I could have found an opening or taken him around the number five and three horses. Star could have won, Mom. It was my fault we came in fourth."

Ashleigh shook her head and swiped at some dirt on Christina's cheek. "It was only your second race, Chris. Don't be too hard on yourself," she said sympathetically. "Getting boxed in is every jockey's nightmare—it happens all the time. You go get cleaned up. I'll start cooling him off."

"I'll help," Christina said, quickly falling into step beside her. The last thing she wanted to do was to go to the jockey room and see George's and Sammy's gloating faces.

Ashleigh halted Star. "No. You go to the jockey room. Dealing with the jockeys after you've raced is something all bugs have to learn to handle."

"You're right," Christina agreed reluctantly.

Ashleigh gave her an encouraging smile, then led Star from the track. Christina took a deep breath. Her mother *was* right. She had to face Sammy and George and hold her head high, no matter what they said. She didn't want to be among the many bugs who couldn't take the pressure and wound up quitting.

You can do it, Christina told herself as she followed behind the other jockeys to the locker room. The riders for the second race were heading out to the viewing paddock.

Christina looked around for Melanie. She spotted her cousin holding a pool cue and talking to Tommy Turner—one of the friendlier journeyman jockeys—as they watched a replay of Christina's race. Sammy and George were right beside them.

Mesmerized, Christina couldn't help but watch along with them. Star seemed to be running smoothly until the fourth furlong, when Christina tried to make her move between Turnabout and Hail to Victory. Suddenly Star's head shot up. That was when George had whacked him, but just as Christina had thought, she couldn't see the whip. The movement made Star fall behind, and as the two horses boxed the colt in, George turned away from the screen and looked at Christina with a smile of triumph on his face.

"Hey, Sammy," Raoul called from across the room. "What were you and George doing in that race? You two were so close together, we thought you were holding hands."

Sammy snickered. "Nah. Me and George were doing a little bug control."

"Extermination," George added with a chuckle.

Turning away, Christina hurried into the women's locker room. When she saw it was empty, she breathed a sigh of relief and plopped onto the bench.

"Chris?" Melanie came into the locker room, still carrying her pool cue. "You okay?"

"Sure." Bending over, Christina began to pull off her boots. "Why shouldn't I be? Jockeys lose every day. And I think I rode well enough that the stewards will take away the conditional approval on my apprentice license."

"Good." Melanie sat down next to her. "I just thought you might be upset 'cause you got boxed in again, except this time it was too late to go wide and pull off a win."

Christina dropped one boot on the floor. "Okay. I'm upset."

"Can I give you a suggestion?"

Christina looked up. "What?"

"Well, when you got boxed in, I knew you were thinking about going to the outside. What you didn't notice was the opening on the inside. Turnabout swerved right toward Victory, leaving an opening by Hornet's Nest, the horse on the rail."

Stunned, Christina just stared at her cousin.

"I know you didn't see it," Melanie rushed on. "I probably wouldn't have, either. I mean, it's easy to watch the replays and see what you *should* have done. When you're in the middle of a race that takes less than two minutes, it's not so easy. But next time don't forget to look for every hole."

Christina put her head in her hands. "Oh, I *really* blew it, didn't I?"

"Hey, don't worry. We all make mistakes."

You don't, Christina wanted to say.

Melanie patted Christina on the shoulder. "I have to go get ready. Will you be okay?" Christina nodded, but as soon as she heard the door shut, she let out a groan. If Melanie had seen Christina's mistake, everybody must have. Brad was sure to insist on a different jockey for Star's next race.

When she had showered and changed, Christina headed for the shed rows. By now Star would be almost cooled off. She'd see how he was, then hurry to the rail to catch Melanie's race.

Dani, one of Whitebrook's grooms, was walking Star around the barn area. A blue-and-white cooler was draped over his back. Christina smiled as Star snorted suspiciously at an overturned bucket, then pranced sideways. The race obviously hadn't worn him out.

"Hi, Dani. How's my boy?" Christina asked. Dani halted Star, and Christina gave the colt an affectionate hug.

"He's yanking my hand off," Dani grumbled good-naturedly. "Sorry you two didn't win. He's sure got the power."

"I know." Christina took the lead from her. "Thanks. I'll finish walking him. Have you seen my dad?"

"He went to help Ian take Wind Chaser to the paddock," Dani explained.

Christina knew that Samantha was disappointed she couldn't be there to watch Wind Chaser, but she and Parker had taken a group of Whisperwood's students to a dressage clinic.

Christina turned Star in the other direction. She wasn't quite ready to face anyone. "I'm sorry I let you down, big guy," she said, lacing her fingers in his mane.

In silence, they walked past the long rows of barns. Several grooms were cooling off their owners' horses. Christina recognized Hornet's Nest, whose neck was still lathered.

After fifteen more minutes, Christina checked under Star's cooler. He was perfectly dry. "Let's go back to the barn. I bet you're hungry."

When she led Star into his stall, he strode inside, checked out his feed bucket, then stuck his head over the door and nickered. Christina scratched the white star on his forehead. "All right. One order of hay coming right up."

As she walked toward the supply stall she could hear Brad's voice coming from inside. "An experienced jockey would have won!" he was saying loudly. Christina stopped about twenty feet from the door.

Holding her breath, she tried to listen in.

"Perhaps," she heard her mother say. "And perhaps Star wouldn't run at all for another jockey."

"That's baloney," Brad retorted. "An experienced jockey knows how to win on any horse. We should have had Tommy Turner or Raoul Menendez on Star. They would have seen that hole. The colt had plenty of fire. They could have ridden him to a win."

"You mean if Tommy or Raoul had been riding, your jockey wouldn't have cracked Star on the nose?" Ashleigh retorted.

Christina gasped. So her mother *had* seen it!

Brad didn't hesitate for a second. "What are you talking about? What are you implying?"

"You're just lucky George's move didn't show up on the replay or I would have protested," Ashleigh insisted.

"If George hit Star, it had nothing to do with me," Brad said indignantly. "You know how jockeys are. They'll do anything to win. Which just proves what I've been saying—Star needs an experienced jockey who can handle these sorts of problems during a race. Don't you agree?"

Christina held her breath, waiting to hear what her mother would say. Just then Ashleigh stepped from the stall carrying a bucket. When she noticed Christina, she froze. Christina saw the guilty expression on her mother's face and knew what her answer would have been.

Turning, Christina raced away from the barn area. Tears pricked her eyes as she wove through the crowd. Finding a spot on the rail, she stared blindly at the empty track, picturing her race in her mind. How had she missed the opening next to Hornet's Nest?

Brad was right. She did need more experience before she could race Star again. She couldn't let him down the way she had during this race.

A race every three weeks was about all a two-year-old could handle. Her parents probably wouldn't enter Star in another race until the end of July. If she raced every weekend for her parents and other trainers, Christina would have a lot more racing experience by the time Star went to the post again.

Good idea, but it will never work, Christina thought glumly.

She had to be realistic. She'd ridden in only two races. She didn't even have an agent. Who would want to hire her? Even her parents would probably prefer to put another jockey on their own horses.

"Here they come!" the announcer called, pulling Christina away from her thoughts. The post parade for the fifth race was already under way.

"Good luck, Mel!" Christina called as Melanie jogged past on Wind Chaser, though she knew her cousin probably couldn't hear her above the noise of the crowd.

Christina leaned over the rail to watch the horses load into the starting gate. This was a mile-and-an-eighth stakes race. Since apprentice jockeys received no weight advantage in a stakes race, Melanie was competing on even ground with the big guys.

The horses loaded quickly, and a hush fell over the crowd.

"It's post time!" the announcer called.

The starter's gun went off, the gates flew open, and the horses leaped onto the track. Melanie and Chaser broke cleanly from the number five position. Immediately Melanie guided Chaser to the rail, behind the two lead horses.

Christina crossed her fingers. "Go, Chaser. Go!"

The field flashed by so fast, Christina only caught a glimpse of Melanie's blue-and-white silks. As they thundered around the bend she strained to hear the announcer. "It's Mandrake in first, followed by Storm-along. Wind Chaser is in third, hugging the rail. Trailing behind, it's Tropical Island in fourth."

The horses flew up the far stretch, and Christina could see Melanie on the rail, still holding third place. It looked as though she had Chaser rated, and he was galloping comfortably.

Christina smiled proudly. Crouched low, Melanie

appeared to know exactly what she was doing. She was positioned perfectly on the rail, waiting to make her move when Mandrake and Stormalong grew tired.

They came around the bend. Again Christina tuned in to the announcer's voice when she lost sight of her cousin.

"As they head toward the homestretch, Mandrake fades. Stormalong is in the lead with Wind Chaser closing. Wait! Here comes Tropical Island, making his play. Jockey Kincaid's using his whip. Tropical Island passes Stormalong, but Wind Chaser is coming on strong. They're neck and neck heading to the wire. Jockey Melanie Graham seems to be asking Wind Chaser for just a little more. Look at that burst of speed! Wind Chaser wins by a length!"

"Yes!" Christina jumped in the air. "We won!"

"Winning time is one minute forty-nine seconds and fifty hundredths. A great time for Wind Chaser!"

Christina hurried from the grandstand to the winner's circle, spotting her mother standing nearby. Christina felt her heart sink as she remembered Brad's words and the look on her mother's face when she'd seen that Christina had heard every word.

"Weren't they great?" Christina asked, forcing a smile.

"Terrific. Melanie was right on the money," Ashleigh said.

They watched as Melanie, Ian, and Wind Chaser posed for the win photo.

"I guess she should be riding Star, huh?" Christina said.

Her mother frowned. "I didn't say that."

Tears filled Christina's eyes. "You didn't have to say it. I knew what you meant. I heard you and Brad talking."

Her mother touched her on the shoulder. "Chris—"

"And I agree with you," Christina went on, cutting her off. "Star could have won. It was my fault he didn't. You don't need decide what to do—I'll decide for you. Star needs a more experienced jockey, so I'm not going to race him anymore!"

4

WITHOUT WAITING TO HEAR HER MOTHER'S REPLY, CHRISTINA turned and pushed her way through the crowd. Then she broke into a run and didn't stop until she reached Star's stall.

She threw open the door, startling him, but when the colt saw it was her, his ears pricked and he whinnied.

"Hey, you," Christina said, wrapping her arms around his neck and sobbing into his soft mane. "Oh, Star. I'm sorry. I have to get better, so that maybe next time I ride you we won't *lose*," she sniffed. "I just hope I *can* get better."

"Chris? Are you in there?"

Christina stiffened. It hadn't taken her mother long to find her.

44

"Yeah."

She heard the door open.

"I need to clear something up," her mother said, coming into the stall. "You misunderstood what I was about to say to Brad. You're going to be a great jockey, Chris. There's no question of that. But I *was* upset after your race. Not because of you, but because it brought back so many awful memories. By now you're beginning to realize how tough jockeys can be. Most aren't like Vicky or Naomi. They'll use any means they have to win. When Brad suggested you didn't have enough experience, I reacted like a mother. I know what George and Sammy did. And it could have been worse. I don't want to see you get hurt."

"You don't have to explain, Mom," Christina said, turning to face her. "I agree. Right now Star needs an experienced jockey. I'm just holding him back."

"No, you're not holding him back." Ashleigh stepped closer and smoothed a strand of hair off Christina's forehead. "It's almost as if you're communicating too well with him. Because you know each other so well, Star feels your every emotion. He feels your indecision and your fear. As soon as you're confident about riding and winning, the two of you will be unbeatable."

"I hope you're right." Christina sighed as her mother hugged her. "But I'm still not going to race him.

At least not until I get more experience."

Ashleigh shook her head and laughed softly. "How'd you get so stubborn?"

"I learned it from you," Christina said with a grin as she pulled away. "What if Melanie rides Star? She's really on a roll."

"Okay, but I'll have to check it out with Mike and Brad. In the meantime we'll stage some mock races at Whitebrook for you, and every weekend you can race one of our horses. How's that sound?"

"Good, but I think I need even more," Christina said. "I mean, I already know all of our horses—I exercise-ride them. I want to ride other trainers' horses."

Ashleigh looked uncomfortable. "I don't know," she protested.

"I know none of the big trainers will hire a bug with no record," Christina said. "So I'm going to start like most jockeys—at the bottom. Every Thursday and Friday I'll come to the track and hustle rides on claimers with the other bugs."

Her mother's brows shot up. "Claimers! Absolutely *not*, Christina Reese," she declared vehemently. "That's the fastest way I know to get hurt. Trainers who run claimers will put you on crazy or half-broken-down horses that no one else will ride."

"But that's exactly the kind of experience I need!" Christina insisted.

Ashleigh shook her head. "No way. No, no, *no*. And don't go asking your father, because he'll say the same thing." She squinted at Christina. "This has nothing to do with *you*. This is common sense. Understand?"

"Yes," Christina muttered. *I understand but I don't agree*, she thought.

"There are plenty of horses at Whitebrook for you to ride," her mother went on. "How about racing Pride next Saturday?"

"That sounds good," Christina allowed. Racing Pride *would* be great experience, but it wouldn't be enough. The only way she could get enough experience—fast—was to ride claimers. She just wouldn't tell her mom and dad.

Her parents rarely entered horses in the low-profile races during the week. They'd never even know if she raced.

"Now let's go congratulate Melanie and Ian. I know Ian's about to burst with happiness," Ashleigh said, turning away.

Closing the stall door, Christina thought back to the last time she had defied her parents, secretly getting her jockey's license. That had worked out for the best, hadn't it?

And this will, too, Christina told herself as she hurried after Ashleigh. It had to.

• • •

"Parker, you've got to help me," Christina whispered, leaning across the table. It was Sunday night, the day after Star's race. Christina, Parker, Kevin, and Melanie had gone out for dinner at the local seafood restaurant. It was the first time the two couples had been out on a date in a long time—practically forever, Christina decided.

Parker stopped buttering a roll and bent toward her. "Why are you whispering?"

Christina nodded at Melanie and Kevin, who were checking out the music selections in the jukebox. "I don't want them to hear."

"Why? Are you going to ask me to marry you or something?" Parker teased.

The question threw Christina off track. "What are you talking about?"

"I'm joking, Chris." Parker laughed, shaking his head. "You need to lighten up. You've been way too serious lately."

"Well, I need to be serious. This is a crisis."

"A crisis, huh?" Parker shoved the tiny roll in his mouth and started to butter another one. Christina quickly told him about her plan to ride claimers during the week at the track.

"If you want to ride goofy horses, Samantha has a couple of two-year-olds who need work," he said.

"I don't need *riding* experience," Christina explained.

"I need *racing* experience. I need to know what to do in a tight spot. I need to learn to stay focused and not let some obnoxious jockey box my horse in. My mom's letting me ride Pride's Heart this Saturday, but one race is not enough."

"So why is it a big secret?"

Christina slumped against the back of the chair. "Well, my parents sort of told me I wasn't allowed to ride claimers."

"Sounds smart."

"But I have to! If I'm going to be a good jockey, I need to learn all the hard stuff—fast—so I can ride Star again."

"So what exactly do you want me to do?"

"Take me to the track on Thursday and Friday mornings. And if anyone asks where we're going, say . . ." She tapped her lip. "Say I'm helping you give lessons at Edgewood Farm."

"No way." Parker shook his head. "I'm not lying to your parents for you, Chris. I'll take you to the track, but you'll have to come up with your own story."

Christina glared at him. "You *would* have to be Mr. Honest," she accused.

"Well, having an expression like that on your face isn't going to do you much good," Parker answered. "And watch out—your face might stay that way."

Christina laughed. Parker was right. He shouldn't

lie for her. She'd just have to come up with something convincing. Her dad would be away at a yearling sale at the end of the week, anyway, and her mom was so busy she probably wouldn't even notice Christina was gone in the mornings.

"And one other thing," Parker said. "When are you going to get your driver's license? You *are* sixteen, you know."

Christina's eyes widened. She'd been so busy getting her apprentice jockey's license, she'd forgotten all about getting her driver's license.

Just then Kevin and Melanie came back, arguing about the songs they'd picked on the jukebox. "Kevin picked this dopey country thing," Melanie complained as she slid into the seat next to Christina.

Melanie was wearing a denim miniskirt, platform sandals, and a black tank top. Kevin was dressed in a plaid shirt, jeans, and cowboy boots. As different as they were, they made a great team.

"Melanie," Christina said, "why haven't we gotten our driver's licenses?"

Melanie shrugged. "Because we have two chauffeurs? And your parents don't have a car we can drive? And we're too busy riding?"

"Getting your license isn't that easy, either," Kevin said. He held up a finger. "One, you've got take a driving course. Two, you have to get your learner's permit.

Three, you have to pass the test. Four, you've got to have a car." He wiggled all five fingers. "Five, you need more money for insurance and gas."

"Hey, I've got money," Melanie protested. "My winnings this spring come to over eight hundred dollars."

"That might buy four tires," Parker joked.

"My parents would probably pitch in. We could buy a car together," Christina told her cousin.

"I can ask my dad to pitch in, too," Melanie added, sounding excited. She turned to face Christina. "Did I tell you that Susan and my dad are coming for a visit?"

"No. When?"

"Sometime in July." Melanie frowned and started poking the ice cubes in her glass with her straw.

Christina knew that Melanie was worried about how her father would react when he found out how much she'd been racing. "You don't seem too excited about their visit."

"I am. It's just my dad has these illusions of me going to art school in New York City or coming to work with him when I graduate. He has no idea how much racing means to me now."

"That's a whole year from now," Parker said. "Look how my plans changed." When Parker had graduated that spring, he'd almost decided to go to a prestigious business college in Italy. But Parker couldn't give up riding—he'd always dreamed of riding in the Olympics.

Christina was glad he'd decided to stay in Kentucky, and she was sure his horse, Foxy, was glad, too.

Melanie shook her head. "I'm never giving up racing. I'd even ride *claimers* if there were no other horses."

Christina shot Parker a don't-say-anything look. She hated to keep Melanie in the dark about her plans. She and her cousin shared just about everything. But if something happened and Christina's parents found out she was riding without permission, she didn't want her cousin to get in trouble, too.

"I hear you're racing Pride Saturday, Chris," Kevin said.

"Yeah. And I hope I do better than I did yesterday."

"Let's toast." Kevin held up his soda glass. "To winning."

"To winning!"

Everyone clinked glasses, but Christina was preoccupied. Which trainers should she approach for rides when she got to the track on Thursday? And what would she say?

Someone will give me a chance. They have to.

5

"OKAY, YOU GUYS, TRY TO BREAK AT THE SAME TIME," ASH-leigh instructed the four riders milling in a group on Whitebrook's track. It was Tuesday, and Ashleigh and Ian had set up a mock race to help Christina practice. "Naomi, you and Fast Gun try to cut Christina off. Kevin, you and Thunder Bones zigzag across the track. Melanie, you and Rascal head for the rail and don't give an inch."

"What am I supposed to do?" Christina asked. Sassy Jazz was jigging in place, eager for a workout. Christina wished she were riding Star, but since he'd raced only three days before, it was too early to work him hard.

Melanie circled Rascal, who chewed on his bit. Since Fast Gun liked to kick, Naomi was keeping him away from the others. Only Thunder Bones stood as quietly as an old school horse, his eyes half closed.

"You need to pretend you're in a real race and figure out what to do on your own," Ashleigh told Christina. "You're going only six furlongs, so you've got to think fast."

Ian nodded. "The idea of this practice is to work on getting out of tricky situations. Don't worry about speed as much as strategy."

"Sounds like fun," Kevin said, fastening the chin strap on his helmet. "Like bumper cars for horses."

"Right. Except horses don't have bumpers," Ashleigh reminded him. "So be careful."

"Let's load 'em," Ian said, taking Rascal's reins.

Goose bumps of excitement prickled Christina's arms.

Christina had drawn the second-place position. When Rascal was loaded, Sassy walked in without hesitation.

As Christina waited for Fast Gun and Thunder Bones to load, she quickly ran through her strategy. Ashleigh had told Melanie to get on the rail and hang there. But Christina would outsmart her cousin and get there first. Rascal wasn't a fast starter. If Christina could get the rail position, she'd be safe from Thunder Bones even if he swerved all over the track. And Naomi would have a tough time trying to get from the fourth gate position to the rail to cut them off.

"That means a fast, clean break," she whispered to Sassy. That was something she definitely needed to work on.

"All loaded," Ian said as he headed for the sidelines.

Christina leaned low over the filly's neck, and Sassy danced in place.

"Post time!" Ian announced as if it were a real race, and then the gun went off.

Sassy leaped from the gate, and Christina pressed her to run even faster so that she could get to the rail position before Melanie. But suddenly Melanie steered Rascal hard to the right, away from the rail and into Sassy. The two horses bumped sides, and Melanie's stirrups clinked against Christina's.

The bump threw off Sassy's stride, and Christina fought to keep control of her head. What was her cousin doing?

By the time Christina had smoothed Sassy out, Kevin and Thunder Bones had cut in front of them and Melanie was on the rail, just where she wanted to be.

Gritting her teeth, Christina hunkered down. "All right, let's show them what we've got."

She set her hands higher on Sassy's crest, urging her faster. Grinning devilishly, Kevin glanced at her over his shoulder, then steered Thunder Bones right in front of her. "Bumper cars!" he whooped, suddenly veering left. "Watch out!"

You watch out, Christina thought. Kevin had left a narrow hole to his left. Christina tugged on the left rein, and Sassy headed for the gap. Just then Melanie swerved right again. But Christina ignored her cousin, urging Sassy on. The game filly blew ahead, but as the fourth furlong pole flashed past, Naomi and Fast Gun seemed to come from out of nowhere.

The pair flew ahead of the dueling pack, streaking past the wire a length ahead of them. When Kevin slowed Thunder Bones, he was laughing.

Christina was not. "What was that all about, Melanie?" she asked as she cantered Sassy beside Rascal. "You were supposed to go to the rail—not bump into us. If this was a real race, you would have been disqualified."

"If it was a real race, I would have bumped you even harder," Melanie declared. "And I doubt a steward would have disqualified me. It was an honest bump made in the heat of the race." She smirked. "Right, Rascal?"

Christina didn't argue. Melanie had outsmarted her. Christina jogged Sassy back to where Ashleigh and Ian were standing along the rail. "We need to do that again—soon," she said. "And next time I'll be ready for their tricks."

Ian chuckled. "Kevin and Melanie tried to cheat, huh? Why am I not surprised?"

"We'll have to wait until next week," Ashleigh said. "Once a week is enough to do something like this. I don't want to press my luck. We're just asking for an accident to happen."

"Once a week!" Christina sputtered. "But that's not nearly enough."

"Don't forget you're racing Pride on Saturday," Ian said. "It's an allowance race for three-year-olds and up. Should be a fast race with lots of good horses."

"Good," Christina said.

But inside she was more convinced than ever that she would have to ride claimers. She only wished she could tell Ian and Ashleigh her plans.

Early Thursday morning Parker dropped Christina off at the backside gate at Churchill Downs. The sun was rising, casting a pink glow on the acres of barns that stretched before her. Christina had been spending time at the Kentucky tracks ever since she was a baby, so she knew most of the trainers' names and reputations. Still, her heart pounded. She'd had no idea that trying to convince one of them to hire her as a jockey would be so scary.

Summoning up her courage, she strode toward the

first row of stalls. "Is Mr. Oakley here?" she asked a groom bathing a gray horse. The girl nodded toward an office door.

Christina took a deep breath before knocking on the doorjamb.

"Whaddaya want?" someone hollered from inside. Christina peeked around the doorway. A heavyset man sat at a desk, filling out forms.

"Hi, Mr. Oakley, I'm Christina Reese, and I was wondering if you needed a jockey for—"

"Nope. Already got enough jocks."

"Both today *and* tomorrow?"

"Yup."

"Well, thank you. And if you should need a—"

"Won't."

"Okay, thanks anyway."

As Christina walked away, she blew out her breath. *That wasn't so bad, now, was it?* she tried to tell herself. But she knew what the real answer was: *Yes, it was awful!*

At the next set of stalls she found the trainer yelling at an exercise boy who was holding the reins of a huge bay Thoroughbred.

"I don't care if his knees are the size of grapefruits," the trainer snapped. "The vet said he can run, and Buckley wants him in Saturday's race. So get on and work him."

The exercise rider gave Christina an apologetic look, then led the horse toward the track.

"What do you want?" the trainer barked at Christina.

"Nothing." She took a step backward. She was desperate to ride, but not that desperate. "I mean, I was looking for June Fortig's stalls," she said quickly.

The trainer jerked his head to the right. "Other side."

Christina nodded dumbly, then whirled and almost ran to the adjacent barn. "Is Ms. Fortig here?" she asked a kid cleaning tack.

"Second stall down."

Christina looked over the top of the Dutch door. A woman was crouched in the straw, unwrapping a horse's leg. "Hi, Ms. Fortig, I'm Christina Reese. Do you need a jockey for—"

"Don't use bugs," she said after giving Christina a hasty glance.

"How did you know I was a bug?"

"I've seen you ride."

"Oh." Christina grimaced. Obviously that was the reason the trainer didn't want her.

"You're not so bad for a bug," the trainer added, her eyes back on the horse's leg. "Why don't you try Phil Oberman? I heard his usual jock tore his knee up. Barn six-A."

"Oh—th-thanks!" Christina stammered, momentarily startled by the trainer's help.

By the time Christina found barn 6A, her palms were sweating. She found Mr. Oberman talking to a client. He was younger than the other trainers—he didn't look much over twenty.

Patiently she waited under the eaves of the shed row for the two men to stop talking. A horse poked his head over the stall partition, and she scratched under its mane.

"Mr. Oberman." She stepped forward when the client left. "I heard you might need a jockey."

He looked her up and down. "You a bug?"

She nodded.

"How much experience?"

Christina gulped. "Two races." Her answer came out in a squeak.

He shook his head. "I'm just starting out, so I've got the rough ones and the young ones. You'll get killed."

"That's okay!" Christina blurted. "I mean, not the killing part. But I need experience on different horses. Tougher horses."

Frowning, he studied her again. "You're Ashleigh Griffen's daughter, aren't you?"

She nodded.

"What're you doing here then? Doesn't Whitebrook have enough horses for you to ride?"

"No. See, if I'm ever going to be a good jockey, I need to ride lots of horses," Christina explained honestly. "Not just the horses I know and grew up with."

Folding his arms, the trainer thought a minute. "Well, my regular jock can't ride, and no one else is beating down my door. I'll try you this afternoon. I've got two claimers. Neither can run, but their owners think they're the next Derby winners."

"I'll do it!" Christina squealed excitedly.

He chuckled. "I've never heard a jock so excited about riding two losers."

Christina ignored his comment. "When are the races? What time do you want me? What are your barn colors? Can I meet the horses?"

"Whoa. One question at a time."

But Christina was too excited. Her plan was going to work. Someone wanted her to ride!

6

"I SHOULD HAVE GUESSED YOU'D BE THE KIND OF JOCKEY who likes to meet your mounts," Mr. Oberman said. "I like that. Too many jocks are only in it for the money."

"Not me," Christina told the trainer. "I want to be good, good enough to win the Kentucky Derby one day." *On Star,* she added to herself.

"How long have you had your apprentice license, anyway?" he asked as they walked toward one of the stalls. "Oh, and call me Phil. I'm not old enough to be Mr. Anything yet."

"Two months."

"*That's* why you're so excited about riding claimers."

Christina followed Phil down the aisle. He stopped in front of a stall, and a small chestnut mare stuck her head over the door. "This is Cat City. If she gets claimed, it'll be a blessing. Her owner's a jerk."

Christina patted the mare's neck. She had a white stripe and a delicate dished face. "She looks pretty enough to be a children's hunter."

"She *should* be a children's hunter." Phil walked down to the next stall. "This is Swept Away. He's an old, banged-up, grouchy gelding. I hope Bill Markham, his owner, will retire him after this year."

Christina peered into the stall. The bay horse stayed in the corner, a bored look on his face. Christina wasn't sure what to say about the two horses she'd be riding. They weren't anything like the expensive stakes horses Ashleigh and Mike trained. But they were exactly what she needed to ride.

"Cat runs in the first race, at eleven o'clock. Swept Away runs in the third race."

"Perfect." She'd be home early enough so her mother wouldn't get suspicious.

As they walked back to the office Phil told Christina more about the two horses. She listened closely. "Any suggestions for the race?"

"Well, if you ride like your mom, you'll figure it out as you go." Phil laughed.

"How do you know my mom?"

"I don't, really. My dad's been training horses forever, so I saw your mom ride when I was a kid. She had quite a reputation, you know. I watched you ride Saturday just out of curiosity."

"And you still want to hire me?" Christina asked, half joking, half serious.

He shrugged. "Sure. I know how hard it is to prove yourself in this business. Nobody wants to give a kid a chance." He checked his watch. "You've got plenty of time until Cat's race. Why don't you gallop a few horses for me? I'll pay you ten bucks a head, and it'll give me a chance to see you ride."

Christina's face broke into a huge grin. "I'd love to. And please give me any tips you can think of."

"Hey, Chris, how come you're slumming with us other bugs?" Fred Anderson asked Christina when she came out of the women's locker room later that morning. Fred was a former high school wrestler who'd decided he wanted to be a jockey. He was strong and athletic, with a barrel chest and broad shoulders but not much experience with horses.

"Slumming?" Christina repeated, not sure what Fred meant, though Phil had said almost the same thing that morning. She glanced around, realizing the jockey room was filled with many of the apprentice jockeys she'd met during the training meetings the stewards held.

"Yeah, slumming," Karen Groves repeated. Karen was a tiny redhead who'd been racing for over a year and still had only two wins. "You know, riding anything with four legs so you can get experience and get noticed."

Christina flushed. "Exactly," she murmured.

Just then the announcer called the first race. Saying goodbye, Christina headed out to the viewing paddock to meet Phil and Cat City. Dark clouds had moved in over the past hour to cover the sun, and the air felt damp. Christina crossed her fingers, hoping it wouldn't rain. Phil had already warned her that Cat didn't like to run in mud. The mare didn't like being jostled, either, and she didn't like dirt hitting her in the face. "Gotta face it—she's a prima donna," the trainer said.

It didn't take long for Christina to discover that racing during the week was definitely different from racing on the weekend. Only a handful of people stood around the viewing paddock, and when she rode Cat City onto the track for the post parade, she noticed the grandstand wasn't even half filled.

But the excitement Christina felt when Cat was loaded into the starting gate was definitely the same.

Phil had also warned her that the petite filly didn't have much interest in working hard enough to win. "That means I'm going to have to sweet-talk you," Christina whispered to Cat, whose ears flicked back and forth. As Christina continued to talk, she made her voice rise higher and higher with excitement. "If we get out front, we won't get dirty. And when you cross the finish line, Phil will have a big, juicy apple for you."

"Sounds great to me," the assistant starter said, laughing. "I'm so hungry, *I'd* even run for an apple."

Minutes later the starter's gun sounded. Cat broke fast and clean from the gate. "Go, girl," Christina urged, keeping the same excitement in her voice. "Show them how tough you are."

Cat's ears continued to flick, so Christina knew she was listening. As they thundered down the track Christina tried to keep the filly away from the other horses so that she wouldn't be bumped or pelted with dirt. At the same time she cajoled and encouraged her.

Her strategy worked. Slowly Cat inched past the field until she was neck and neck with a dark bay named Love Struck. Christina shot the bay a sidelong glance. Fred was hunkered on the filly's neck, pumping with his hands. When he saw Christina gaining, he raised his whip. Instantly Love Struck flattened her ears and rolled back one eye, clear signals that she hated to be hit. Fred whacked her anyway, and Love swerved sideways away from the stick and into the rail. Then Cat surged ahead, crossing the finish line a length ahead of the others.

"Woo!" Christina pumped a fist in the air. "We did it!"

When Phil met them outside the winner's circle, he was beaming from ear to ear. "That's the fastest this filly has ever run!" he declared as Christina dismounted to get weighed. "And you know what the best news is?" He glanced around as if making sure no one could hear, then whispered to Christina, "I convinced a friend of mine who trains and shows hunters to put a claim on her. Cat's going to a new home!"

"Wow! That is good news," Christina repeated, feeling giddy herself. Not only had she won, but the race had been fun. Now everybody—trainers, riders, handlers, and officials—seemed friendlier, and Christina felt less tense.

Mom was wrong, Christina decided as she took the saddle and headed for the scales. *Riding claimers is exactly what I need.*

When the photos were finished, Christina went back to the jockey room to wait for her race on Swept Away. "Nice job!" several of the bugs congratulated her when she came in and watched the replay with them.

"I told Fred he shouldn't use the whip on Love Struck," Karen said. "But did he listen? No."

"I'm glad he *didn't* listen," Christina said, still grinning. For the next hour she played pool and bantered with the other jockeys and bugs. Even though they were competing with each other, the atmosphere seemed lighter. George, Sammy, and many of the other veterans weren't there, and Christina didn't miss them at all.

When it was time for her race on Swept Away, Christina hurried outside with Karen, who was riding in that race, too. It was raining.

"Do you think they'll cancel the race?" Karen asked, glancing at the sky.

"No way. My horse is a mudder, anyway," Christina said confidently. "So he should be all right."

When they reached the paddock, Christina wished Karen good luck. The tiny bug was riding number four, a nasty-looking brown gelding called Storm Trooper, who pinned his ears at the other horses. One of Karen's problems was handling the bigger, strong-willed horses. Many accidents happened when bugs lost control of their mounts. Christina hoped Karen could keep Storm Trooper under control.

"Just the kind of race Swept Away likes," Phil said when he led the rangy bay into the saddling stall. "He should do well, *if* he can stay sound." Frowning, he threw the number blanket over the gelding's bony back.

"If?" Christina furrowed her brow. "Is he all right?"

"He's as all right as I can make him," Phil grumbled. "Markham, his owner, wants him to race, and the vet says he's racing sound, so I don't have much choice."

Christina ran her hand down Swept Away's neck,

her earlier excitement fading. This was all part of riding claimers, too, she realized, so she'd better learn to handle it.

Phil led Swept Away from the stall. Christina walked beside the trainer, listening to his instructions, raindrops tapping the top of her helmet. "He breaks slow, then gradually gains momentum. He'll need lots of warming up to get all the creaks out of his joints. Think you can handle it?"

Christina nodded. "This will be the first time I've raced in the rain, though," she said, slightly worried.

"All it'll do is slow the pace. Which will be good for Swept Away. He's slow but steady, and nothing rattles him."

Phil gave her a leg up. As she settled on the damp saddle, Christina felt the familiar anxiety returning. This wasn't going to be as fun as racing Cat, she knew. But riding in the rain was an experience she needed, too.

"Sky's going to open up," Jake, the pony rider, told Christina as he escorted her onto the track. Christina nodded. Already Swept Away's black mane was dusted with droplets of rain. When Christina saw the track surface, she was glad she'd brought several pairs of goggles. The top layer of the track was starting to get slick, which meant the galloping horses would be kicking up a lot of slop and dirt.

Jake stayed beside them as they cantered clockwise, warming up. When they reached the starting gate, he wished Christina good luck. She continued to jog Swept Away in a large circle, trying to keep his muscles loose until they loaded. They'd drawn the seventh slot in a field of seven, which meant Swept Away didn't have to stand in the chute, getting wet and stiff, while the other horses loaded. It also meant Christina could keep him to the outside of the field and away from flying mud.

"It's just you and me, buddy," Christina told Swept Away when they were finally in the stall. He stood so calmly, Christina wasn't sure he'd be ready to break.

The gun sounded. "They're off!" the announcer hollered.

Christina grabbed a hunk of mane, not sure what to expect. Swept Away seemed to break in slow motion. Head down, he bounded forward, heavy on his forehand, as if he were running uphill. Christina kept her right rein taut, trying to keep him away from the dirt thrown up by the number six horse, who was just ahead of them.

Shifting her weight back, she collected her mount. Then she put her hands on his crest and pumped, pushing him on with her voice and body. Swept Away rocked back on his hindquarters, lengthening his stride, and as they rounded the first bend, Christina realized they were keeping pace with the two leaders on the rail.

Then her goggles misted up, and she couldn't see anything. "I need windshield wipers!" she muttered, pulling down the top pair of goggles to reveal another pair underneath. Seconds later they, too, were blurred as the rain slanted into her face. Christina clenched her teeth, frustrated, but she knew the other jockeys were in the same fix.

Half blind, Christina steered the best she could. Fortunately, the pace was slow. Christina was soon down to her last pair of clear goggles. Quickly she assessed the situation. They were heading down the homestretch, the horses strung in a ragtag line. Swept Away, Storm Trooper, and the number two horse were in the lead. The others weren't far behind, but the mud being flung into their faces was taking its toll.

Gradually, without any fanfare, Swept Away pulled ahead of the field. By then Christina couldn't see at all. Reaching up, she took off the last pair of goggles. Fat drops stung her eyelids and nose, but she could see better without the goggles. Swept Away was galloping past the last pole on his way to the wire.

Christina glanced to her left. Karen was crouched over Storm Trooper's neck, her fingers gripping the brown mane as if she were hanging on for dear life. The big horse's nostrils were flared, his neck was flat, his eyes hollow. Storm Trooper was flagging, but Swept Away was still running strong.

71

"We're going to do it!" Christina exclaimed excitedly, her voice carrying over Storm Trooper's labored huffing and the rushing rain.

Suddenly she felt Swept Away bobble. It was just a hint of a misstep, but since his pace had been so steady and strong, warning bells rang inside Christina's head.

She glanced down, saw his right shoulder drop with each stride, and knew something was wrong.

Sitting back, she pulled him to a jerky halt. The rest of the horses flew past. Christina jumped off the gelding's back, falling on her knees in the mud. Swept Away pulled back on the reins, dragging Christina with him. She scrambled to her feet, still holding tightly to the reins.

"Whoa," she said firmly. Stumbling forward, she tried to stay with him as he hobbled backward. "Whoa. Easy, buddy."

Swept Away finally stopped, his front leg cocked at an awkward angle. Christina's heart fell. He was hurt!

7

CHRISTINA BEGAN TO CRY, HER TEARS MIXING WITH THE beating rain. "I'm so sorry," she said, her hands cupped around Swept Away's muzzle.

Phil jogged up, a lead line in his hand. "What happened?"

"His right leg."

Phil stooped and ran his hands from knee to hoof. "Feels like a bow, not a break," he said. Just then the track veterinarian hurried over. Christina stepped aside, watching as the two checked Swept Away's leg. The gelding's head hung low, and his breathing was shallow, as if he was in pain.

Christina felt miserable.

After a few minutes the vet pulled a special support bandage from his kit and wrapped it around the leg. By that time, the track's horse ambulance and trailer had pulled up.

Hooking the lead to the bit, Phil clucked to Swept Away and gently tugged. Christina watched as Swept Away limped up the ramp and into the trailer. Phil and the vet climbed in with him. Two workers secured the back trailer door, and they drove away.

One of the gate crew tapped Christina on the shoulder. "You'd better get off the track, miss," he said. "They're going to harrow it for the next race."

Christina nodded numbly. She was soaked. Wrapping her arms around her chest, she followed the workers and officials out the gate. This time when she reached the jockey room, no one congratulated her. Everybody wanted to know what had happened, but Christina didn't know what to say. *What* did *happen out there?* she wondered as she stumbled into the locker room. Was it something she could have avoided? Had it been her fault?

She showered and dressed, feeling better once she was dry. Packing her wet clothes in her gym bag, she headed out the locker room door. Karen was standing with the other jockeys, chattering excitedly as they watched a replay of the race. Until then Christina hadn't even realized that Storm Trooper had won.

Everyone was silent when the camera focused on Christina and Swept Away. Seconds after the gelding took the bad step, Christina had pulled him up. It was only yards before the finish line. She gulped. There were all sorts of rules about stopping a horse too early. Would Phil still want her to ride for him if she made such stupid mistakes?

"Congratulations, Karen," Christina called before leaving to see how the gelding was doing.

Phil was waiting outside. As soon as Christina saw him, her eyes filled with tears again.

"Is Swept Away okay?" she asked as she hurried up to him.

He nodded. "Thanks to you."

Christina stopped in her tracks. "Me?"

"You saved his life. If you hadn't pulled him up when you did, he probably would have fractured his leg. The bow was nasty, but it will heal."

Christina didn't know whether to feel relieved or not. "Was his owner mad that I pulled him up before finishing the race?"

Phil shrugged. "He started to bluster, but I told him you did the right thing."

"What about Swept Away? Will he ever race again?"

"Never," Phil declared solemnly. Christina was crestfallen, but Phil chucked her lightly on the shoulder. "Don't feel so bad. Believe it or not, Markham's got a soft spot for the old horse. He's retiring Swept Away to his daughter's farm."

"Great!" Christina choked down the sob that welled in her throat. "Well, almost great," she added softly. "My first race in the rain, and look what happens. Disaster."

"It wasn't your fault. Swept Away was a bow waiting to happen," Phil reassured her. "Still want to race claimers?"

No, Christina almost blurted. But then she caught herself. Even stakes winners broke down. With horses, there were no guarantees.

She smiled. "Yes. But do you still want me to jockey for you?"

"You bet. I've got two horses entered tomorrow, so I'll see you bright and early. Then next week we move to Ellis Park." He cocked his head. "My regular jockey won't be ready by then. Still game?"

Christina nodded. "Definitely."

That night Christina was so exhausted she could barely hold her head up during dinner. Melanie had gone to watch Kevin play in a baseball tournament, so Ashleigh had fixed scrambled eggs and muffins for the two of them. When she came into the kitchen for dinner, it was the first time she'd seen her mother all day.

Christina dropped into a kitchen chair, propped her

head on one hand, then spoke the question she'd been waiting all day to ask. "How was Star's workout this morning?"

"Not bad," her mom said as she handed Christina a plate of eggs. "Star's not running his best, but Melanie tried hard. I think she'll do a good job in the next race."

"I hope so." Christina yawned.

Her mother gave her a curious look, then slid into the chair across from her. "You look tired. Did the little kids wear you out?"

"Kids?" Christina repeated, momentarily puzzled. "Oh, uh, yeah." She'd almost forgotten the story she'd told her mother about teaching at the clinic. "Standing around in the rain and resetting a thousand jump courses and fence poles was kind of tiring," Christina went on, making the morning sound so real, she could almost picture herself at Edgewood Farms. "I don't know how Mona and Sam give riding lessons week after week."

"I hope you won't be too worn out to ride Pride this Saturday," her mother commented.

"I'm never too tired to race." Christina reached for her glass of milk. "And it'll be fun racing at Ellis Park. It'll be my first time."

"It's too bad this clinic came at such an awkward time." Ashleigh passed Christina the basket of muffins.

"You could have breezed a few horses on Ellis Park's track tomorrow morning."

Christina felt her cheeks redden. "Um, well, I've got the race Saturday, and next week I'll gallop horses *every* day. Maybe Ian will put me on Fast Gun," she added. "He's a handful."

"I don't think you're ready for him yet." Pulling up the sleeve of her T-shirt, Ashleigh pointed to her upper arm. Christina's eyes widened. There were two sets of teeth marks in the bruised flesh.

"Ouch!" Christina straightened. "What happened?"

"Fast Gun bit me. He's getting to be as bad as Terminator."

Terminator was one of Whitebrook's stallions. He was so aggressive, only George Ballard, the stallion manager, handled him. Early in life Christina had learned to give Terminator and his stall a wide berth.

"The other day Fast Gun went after Joe and tried to trample him," Ashleigh continued. "We've discovered he doesn't like men."

Christina couldn't help giggling. "Maybe you'd better quit wearing jeans and use more perfume."

"He was going after Jonnie, if you must know," Ashleigh said, laughing. "I happened to be in his way. He's got a mean streak, that's for sure. I told Kimberley McFarland, his owner, that if she wants to keep running him, he should be gelded. That way he'll keep his mind on racing instead of eating people. She doesn't want to, though, until the season slows. So until then we'll have to watch out."

"I'm glad Star's a sweetie."

Ashleigh arched one brow. "Actually, he gave Melanie a funny look this morning, right before she got on him."

Christina stopped chewing. "What kind of a look?"

"As if he was telling her, 'I don't want you on my back, but I'm too much of a gentleman to be mean about it.'"

"Uh-oh." Christina remembered when Star was a yearling at Townsend Acres. He'd gotten coltish and aggressive, and had been severely punished by Brad's trainer. "I'll have a talk with Star tonight."

"You do that," Ashleigh said matter-of-factly, and Christina knew that her mom understood that she really *would* have a talk with him, as crazy as it sounded.

"Did Dad call?"

"Yes. He's found two yearlings he really likes. They have great bloodlines...."

While Ashleigh chatted about the phone call, Christina's mind wandered. She wished she could tell her mom all about her day at the track. Even though she would rather have been riding Star, it had been exhilarating in its own way.

Except for Swept Away. Just thinking about the gelding made Christina's eyes fill with tears. *Poor boy.*

"Chris? Honey? Are you all right?"

Her mother's concerned voice broke into her thoughts.

"Yeah, fine," Christina blurted, scooping up the last of her eggs. "I'm so tired my eyes are tearing. After I see Star, I'm going to bed. I've got another early day at the, uh, clinic tomorrow."

Standing, Ashleigh started to clear the table. "I'll clean up. It's late, so don't stay with Star too long."

"I won't." Jumping up, Christina gave her mom a hug, wishing she could share her sadness—and happiness—with her. Ashleigh looked momentarily puzzled, but Christina hurried out to the mud room before she could say anything.

She slipped into an old pair of sneakers before heading out the door. The night was muggy after the rain, and the sound of tree frogs filled the air. There was a full moon behind the clouds, so the sky was bluish gray, and the barns were bathed in the warm glow of the outside vapor lights.

Since Star didn't have a race for two weeks, he was turned out in a small paddock to graze. Christina jogged to the paddock. Opening the gate, she whistled, and the colt trotted over, ducking his head to check her pockets for a carrot.

80

"Not tonight," Christina said. She ran her hand down his neck, which was gritty with dirt. "Did you roll?"

He rubbed his forehead against her arm.

"Hey. Show some respect," Christina scolded softly. "I'll scratch it for you, but don't push me around. If Brad ever saw you acting like Fast Gun, he'd jump at the chance to take you back to Townsend Acres." She lowered her voice, sounding ominous. "And you know what that means. Ralph Dunkirk."

Star pawed the ground and snorted as if he understood.

"You remember him, I know." Turning, Christina closed the gate and climbed up on the top board of the fence. Star nibbled at the toe of her tennis shoes and then lowered his head to graze.

"Wait, I'm not through with you." Leaning forward, Christina tapped him on the withers. "You've got to be nice to Melanie."

She twined her fingers in the colt's mane. "I can't ride you, because I'm riding for Phil. He's a good trainer. Maybe his horses aren't as special as you, but he treats them well."

Christina fell silent a moment, thinking how fortunate she'd been to find Phil. She was pretty sure her mom and dad would say it was okay for her to ride for him. If they knew.

"So do we have a deal?" She turned her attention

back to Star. "You're going to be nice to Melanie, right? Especially on Monday, when Brad will be watching."

Ignoring her, Star moved to another clump of grass.

"And I'm going to ride Phil's horses and get better and better," she added. Star's next race was only two weeks away. "Just please give Melanie a chance."

"Pride likes the jockey to really rate him," Ashleigh instructed Christina as they walked together to Ellis Park's viewing paddock. Churchill Downs had closed for the summer, and the Kentucky racing schedule would continue at Ellis Park from the end of June until the first week in September.

"When you break, take hold of him," Ashleigh continued. "Really rate him until the homestretch, but don't let him get behind. With ten horses running, the field's going to be too congested to try to make a run from behind."

Christina nodded solemnly. Her mother obviously didn't want her to make the same mistakes she had on Star.

"Then show him the whip and let him know it's time to make a move."

The Opening Stakes was a popular race. When Christina and Parker had checked out the *Daily Racing Form* that morning, she'd realized just how prestigious the race was. The field consisted of ten colts with good pedigrees and racing records, and except for Christina, the jockeys were experienced.

"I'll do my best," Christina said. "Thank you for giving me this chance."

Her mother smiled. "We're not taking a chance. We believe in you, Chris."

Christina smiled and headed into the busy paddock.

Mike was there, holding Pride in the saddling stall. The bay colt looked serenely handsome. He didn't have Star's fire and personality, but he'd developed into a powerful racehorse.

"Any instructions, Dad?" Christina asked when she handed Mike her saddle. He smoothed the number five blanket before setting the saddle on the colt's withers.

"You've got a lot of good horses to worry about," Mike said.

"I know. Parker and I went over the *Racing Form* this morning. Tommy Turner's riding Fool's Honor. He beat Pride last year in an allowance race. And Raoul Menendez is on Bayside, that colt who's been doing so well in California."

"Right." Mike went over to Star's other side to make sure the blanket was straight.

"Are you worried?" Christina probed when her dad came back around. "I know it's the first time I've ridden against so many good horses."

Mike shot her a cocky grin. "Nah. I know you can do it."

Minutes later Christina and Pride paraded onto the track. Once again she noticed the difference between weekday and weekend races. Friday she'd raced one filly for Phil. At noon it had started raining again, and the Churchill Downs grandstand had been almost empty. The filly she'd been riding, Lucky Lady, hated mud, so when they placed third, Phil had been happy enough.

But Ellis Park was packed for its opening day. Crowds of people milled along the railings. The grandstand seats and boxes were filled with well-dressed onlookers. Families with lawn chairs and picnic blankets dotted the infield. A huge banner welcoming the fans stretched along the low-slung roof of the grandstand. Everything seemed to sparkle in the sunlight.

Christina smiled, glad she was part of the track's opening day. "Let's show the crowd that Whitebrook's horses are the best!" she told Pride as he broke into an easy canter.

As they cantered toward the starting gate the older colt radiated a calm confidence that made Christina's smile widen. A five-year-old was so much stronger and more coordinated than a two-year-old. This was going to be a great race.

It seemed to take forever to get the ten horses loaded. Pride waited quietly, though Christina could feel the tension in his muscles. Because it was opening day, the announcer took forever telling the crowd about the horses and their jockeys. Christina's ears turned red when he casually mentioned she was the only apprentice jockey racing.

Finally the gun went off. Pride broke smoothly. Following her mother's advice, Christina kept a taut rein. She also kept her eye on the horses galloping on both sides of her. She *wasn't* going to be left behind!

Level with the lead horses, they were in the perfect position. Christina flexed her fingers, nonverbally telling Pride to gallop easily. Her body was low and still on his neck as she waited to make her move. The race was a mile and a half. They had plenty of time.

Packed tightly, the field galloped up the backstretch. As they rounded the final turn, several horses tired and fell behind. Christina glanced to her right and left. Four racehorses were still ahead of her in the lead. Roundabout, a lanky black colt, was in front on the rail. The *Racing Form* had predicted he'd start fast, then burn out. So far he'd led the mile-and-a-half race all the way.

Christina noted Roundabout's flat stride, outstretched, head and puffing nostrils. His jockey was no longer rating him. That meant the colt was about finished. As soon as Roundabout began to lag she'd steer Pride to the rail.

On her right, Fool's Honor, ridden by Tommy Turner, was closing fast. Tommy was riding with a tight rein, which meant that that Honor still had plenty of fire. Christina needed to keep her eye on the chestnut, since Tommy would probably steer toward the rail when he got the chance.

Next Christina listened hard, straining her ears above the noise of pounding hooves and raspy breathing. As the announcer called out the horses' positions to the crowd, he told her what she needed to know. The rest of the field was behind Roundabout, Pride, and Fool's Honor. Bayside, ridden by Raoul, was gaining. That meant that as they headed for the finish line, she only had three horses to worry about.

Down the homestretch they thundered, and Roundabout began to drop back. Christina tugged on the left rein, steering Pride to the rail.

An instant later Bayside pulled alongside her, wedging himself between Pride and Fool's Honor. Neck and neck the three horses galloped down the homestretch. Setting her hands on Pride's crest, Christina pumped with her upper body. "Go, Pride. You can do it!"

She waved the whip by the side of his face, just so he could see it, then urged him on with everything she had. She felt the colt respond, pulling ahead of the other two horses. But she also heard the roar of his breathing. He was giving his all.

At the last second Tommy whacked Fool's Honor on the shoulder with his whip, and the other horse drew alongside Pride. The two sprinted past the finish line, neck and neck, stride for stride.

Christina caught her breath. It was a photo finish!

"What a terrific race on this beautiful opening day," the announcer concluded above the excited roar of the crowd, "with Pride's Heart and Fool's Honor battling to the very end."

Christina pulled Pride up to a jog, watching the board for the final results. She crossed her fingers on the reins.

"And the results are in, folks. In the Opening Stakes, it's Fool's Honor by a nose," the announcer called, "with Pride's Heart in second place. Bayside is a close third."

For a second Christina's heart sank. Second place! But then she caught herself. *Second is okay,* she told herself as she eased Pride to a trot. If the race had been any longer, Pride would have burned out. His nostrils were flared, his sides heaved, and his neck glistened with sweat. He had given the race everything he had, running hard and clean. Even if they hadn't won, Christina was proud of the job she'd done.

At the rail, Parker and Christina's parents were waiting to meet her. They looked happy. Pride had done his best, and Christina had one more race under her belt. One more race toward becoming the kind of jockey who could ride Star to victory.

8

"COME ON, DAD," CHRISTINA PROTESTED THAT NIGHT. "IF Melanie and I can race a thousand-pound horse around a track at forty miles an hour, we can certainly drive a car!"

Reaching for a slice of pizza, Mike gave her a dubious look. On the way home from Ellis Park, Parker and Christina had stopped at a pizza place to pick up something to eat. After the day's races, no one wanted to cook, but everyone was starving.

Now Melanie, Christina, Parker, Ashleigh, and Mike were sitting around the kitchen table with two extra-large pizzas in front of them.

"It's not the same," Mike stated, extracting a slice of pepperoni from the pie. "In the first place, you'll only have your learner's permit, so one of us will still have to drive with you. Then our insurance will go up, and then we'll have to get you a car to drive, and then we'll worry every time you go anywhere." Dropping the slice on his paper plate, he began to massage his temples. "Every father's nightmare."

"Ignore your father," Ashleigh said, nibbling her slice of vegetarian pizza. "You guys do need to learn to drive. That way we won't have to drive you everywhere—what luxury."

"Hey, you guys can start chauffeuring *me* everywhere," Parker chimed in. "It's about time."

"Melanie, does your father know about this?" Mike asked.

Melanie wrinkled her nose. "Yeah. He mentioned the same things you did, Uncle Mike. He even used the word *nightmare*."

Everyone laughed.

Reaching across the table, Ashleigh handed out napkins to everyone. "Monday we'll go get your learner's permits," she told Melanie and Christina. "Okay, you two?"

Christina and Melanie nodded happily.

"Sounds great to me," Melanie said. "And maybe I could even pick Susan and Dad up at the airport next weekend. You'd be with me, of course, Uncle Mike."

Mike let out a loud groan. "No way will I let you drive to the airport. That place is a madhouse!"

"Too bad your father won't be here to watch you race Star," Christina said.

Melanie grimaced. "Maybe it's just as well."

"What does that mean?" Christina noticed her mom and dad exchanging glances. "What? What happened?"

"Star's been giving Melanie some trouble," Mike explained. "Nothing she can't handle, though," he added quickly.

"Trouble?" Christina repeated. "Like what?"

Melanie waved her slice of pizza in the air. "It's *nothing*," she said impatiently. "We're doing fine. I won two races today at Ellis Park on harder horses than Star. Don't worry."

"Don't forget, Brad's coming to watch her gallop Star first thing Monday morning," Ashleigh reminded Christina with a frown.

"Don't worry. I'll be there," Christina said, feeling worried. She knew Melanie was a good rider. But Star could be temperamental. A pang of guilt gripped her. Since she'd been racing these past three days, she hadn't had much time for Star. Was that what was bothering him?

Monday morning Christina finishing painting Star's hooves with hoof oil and stood up. She stepped back to survey her handiwork. Arching his neck, the colt pricked his ears and stood squarely, as if posing for a photo. He was gleaming from head to toe.

"Show-off," Christina teased as she dropped the hoof oil in the grooming box. "Although you are pretty handsome."

"Are you still fussing over that horse?" Melanie asked as she came down the aisle. Since she'd already ridden two horses that morning, she was wearing her helmet and chaps and carrying her exercise saddle.

"It's called grooming," Christina joked. "Or did you forget? I don't think I've seen you pick up a brush in a while. I guess you've been too busy winning races."

"That's what grooms like you are for." Laughing, Melanie plopped her saddle in Christina's arms.

"If it were any other horse, I'd make you tack him up yourself," Christina grumbled jokingly. "You're getting a fat head."

Melanie unhooked the crossties to bridle Star. "Just because I'm winning a lot doesn't mean I have a fat head." Melanie rapped on her helmet. "Though this thing is getting tight."

"Just keep winning," Christina said as she smoothed the pad under the saddle. "Star needs a win. And besides, the more purse money you make, the faster we can get a car. I feel bad asking Parker to drive me everywhere."

"Like to the *clinic* at *Edgewood* last week?" Melanie

asked as she slipped the bridle over Star's ears, then buckled the throat latch. "How come you never told me about it?"

Christina's cheeks grew hot. "Why would I? It was for kids. I didn't think you'd be interested."

"But you never even mentioned it." Melanie gave Christina a suspicious look. "Don't you think that's kind of weird?"

Christina ignored her cousin, walking around Star's rump to his other side to make sure that the girth wasn't twisted before she tightened it.

"Chris," Melanie accused, "are you keeping something from me?"

"If I am, it's for your own good," Christina stated flatly.

Melanie looped the reins over Star's head. "So something *is* going on," she said in a dramatic voice. "Come on, tell me. What are you hiding?"

Christina adjusted Star's girth. "I'll tell you tonight, Mel. After I talk to my parents."

Melanie's brows shot up. "You've been doing something behind your parents' backs?"

Christina nodded. It sounded so terrible when Melanie said it like that, which was why Christina had decided that if she was going to ride for Phil later that week, she had to confess to her parents. She couldn't keep claiming that she was giving lessons at some clinic.

"I didn't tell you because I didn't want you to get into trouble, too," Christina explained. "Especially not when your dad and Susan are coming. Just give Star a great ride. Okay?" Christina pleaded.

"All right, Chris." Melanie shook her head. "But promise you'll tell me tonight?"

"Promise," Christina vowed. "Ready to go?" Melanie nodded, and Christina led Star down the aisle.

"Now remember, he doesn't like you to push too hard with your body," she told Melanie as they walked together. "Use lots of voice, keep him—"

"Chris, I've been riding Star all week," Melanie said, sounding annoyed.

"I just thought I'd give you some tips, since you've been having trouble."

"But it's not like I can't handle him," Melanie said defensively. When they got outside, Melanie took the reins. "Just give me a leg up."

Christina boosted her cousin into the saddle. When Melanie gathered the reins, Star stared at Christina questioningly, his ears flicking back and forth. "I know it's not me riding you, but I'll be on the rail watching," she told him as he nuzzled her neck.

"Don't worry, Chris, we'll do great," Melanie reassured her before turning Star toward Whitebrook's oval. Christina walked beside them, biting her lip when she saw Brad standing with her parents by the rail. *Be good, Star,* she urged silently.

Mike strode over, a stopwatch in his hand. "We'll time you for six furlongs, Melanie. Canter him easy about two furlongs, then let him go. Does that sound okay to you?" he asked Brad, who had followed him over and was walking slowly around Star, studying him.

Brad nodded. "Fine with me."

"It's fine with *me,* too," Melanie chimed.

Way to go, Mel. Christina grinned and gave her cousin a thumbs-up sign. Melanie's eyebrows lifted beneath the brim of her helmet. "Any last-minute instructions, boss?" she asked Christina.

"Just let him do his thing," Christina said, biting back a smile. Star stretched out his nose to nuzzle Christina's shoulder. "Show them what you can do," she told the colt, pushing him gently away. Then she hurried over to the rail, standing a few feet apart from where Brad, Ashleigh, and Mike were huddled together.

Melanie trotted Star clockwise around the outer rail to warm him up. "Good," Ashleigh called to her. "He seems more relaxed today than he did last week."

Christina didn't say anything. She could tell by Star's ears that he *wasn't* relaxed. One ear was tilted forward, but the other was cocked back. Christina knew what that look meant. Star was confused and nervous and unsure of himself.

When Melanie trotted past Christina, she said, "He does feel better. Must be your TLC this morning."

I hope. Christina watched Star head away from her. He was trotting briskly, but he was flicking his tail back and forth in annoyance.

When they reached the other side of the track, Melanie walked Star to the inside rail and turned him counterclockwise. Then she leaned forward and urged him into a canter. The colt leaped forward so abruptly, Melanie fell back, landing hard in the saddle and losing her grip on the reins. Before she could regain her balance, Star was galloping out of control down the track.

Christina grimaced. *Not a good start.* She glanced sideways at Brad, who was frowning angrily.

By the time Melanie regained her balance and picked up the reins, Star was tearing around the far turn. Christina had never seen him run so fast. Melanie was trying to rate him, but the colt ignored her. His nostrils were flared, his expression determined.

When they blew past, Christina could see how frightened her cousin was. Melanie was leaning back in the saddle, sawing on the reins, but her efforts did nothing to slow Star down. He had to be stopped before he hurt himself!

Christina vaulted over the railing, stumbling in the soft footing. "Star, whoa!" she shouted. As Christina ran toward them, Melanie hauled hard on the right rein, trying to force Star's head and body in a circle to the right.

Suddenly Star slid to a dead stop. Melanie flew over his head, somersaulting to the ground.

Christina's heart skipped a beat. "Melanie!" she screamed.

Shaking his head, Star bucked playfully, then trotted toward Christina. When she ran past him, he wheeled and trotted after her. Mike and Ashleigh ran onto the track, with Brad following at a brisk walk.

Christina fell to her knees beside Melanie. She'd taken off her helmet and was holding both sides of her head.

"Are you all right?"

Melanie blinked, then looked around in confusion. "Where am I?"

"At Whitebrook!" Christina answered, alarmed. Did Melanie have a concussion? Had she lost her memory?

"I know *that*. I mean, what am I doing in the dirt? A second ago I was riding that, that—crazy beast!" She pointed an accusing finger at Star, who stood right behind Christina, snuffling her hair.

Christina blew out a relieved breath. Her cousin was all right.

"Melanie!" Ashleigh gasped as she raced up. "What happened? Are you okay? Should we take you to the hospital?"

"I don't know what happened. I think I'm okay," Melanie said. "Nothing's hurt. Well, nothing except my big fat ego."

With Ashleigh's help, Melanie stood up. Christina handed Star's reins to her father. "Do you think Star's okay?" she asked, running her hands down the colt's front legs.

"Seems to be. He's not even winded," Mike said.

"That horse is *nuts*," Brad interrupted. "He could have killed someone." He shook his finger in Christina's face. "And it's all your fault!"

Christina's jaw dropped. "My fault?"

"Yes. You and the so-called bond you have with that horse are an excuse for turning him into a spoiled brat. He's going to hurt someone unless he gets discipline instead of *kisses*." Brad said the word with such disgust that Christina had to pinch her lips together to keep from laughing in his face.

"There's no reason to criticize Christina. She had nothing to do with Melanie's fall," Ashleigh put in, cutting Brad's tirade short. "Melanie, do you remember what was going on before you got thrown?"

Melanie shook her head in confusion. "I turned him, squeezed him with my heels, and *bam*—he took off like he'd been stung by hornets. He was so lazy last week, I guess I just wasn't ready for it." Melanie eyed Star with trepidation. "I think he got it in his head to run away

98

with me. As far as he was concerned, I wasn't even there. He just went."

"He did that, for sure." Mike held out the stopwatch. "He ran the six furlongs in a minute ten seconds."

Brad frowned. "Are you sure you timed him right?"

Mike nodded. "Not that it's any surprise. We know he's fast."

Brad snorted. "Fast means nothing if no one can control him." He turned to Ashleigh. "Obviously Melanie isn't the right jockey for Star."

"I can ride him!" Melanie said indignantly.

Brad ignored her. "It's time you all listened to me. Star is entered in the Debutante Stakes. It's a big race, and he ought to have a suitable rider. Melanie's good, but she's still a bug. We need a jockey who can make him run *and* control him. A jockey *I* choose."

"Melanie can control him," Christina defended her cousin.

"Oh, really?" Brad said sarcastically.

"Brad's right," Mike said, to Christina's surprise. "Melanie, I'm sorry. You're a good rider and a smart jockey, but you and Star aren't clicking."

Melanie ducked her head, her cheeks bright red, but she nodded in silent agreement.

"How about Naomi?" Christina suggested desperately.

Ashleigh shook her head. "Naomi's riding in Virginia that week."

"Then what about Vicky Frontiere?"

Brad crossed his arms over his chest. "She's all booked up. I guess you'll just have to take my choice. I've already mentioned it to George."

Christina gasped. "George!"

"I have a better solution," Ashleigh said so quickly that Christina knew her mother must have been as horrified as she was at the thought of George riding Star.

"What?" Christina and Mike demanded in unison.

Ashleigh's face broke into a grin. "Why don't *I* ride Star in his next race?"

9

CHRISTINA WAS SO STARTLED THAT FOR A MOMENT SHE STARED at her mother, speechless. "*You* want to be Star's jockey?" she asked finally.

"Yes," Ashleigh said, her smile widening. "It hasn't been that long since I raced. I ride almost every day, so I'm in shape. My chiropractor will probably kill me, but if it's just this one race . . . "

Christina continued to stare at her mother. By the expression on her father's face, she could tell he was just as surprised.

"I think it's a good idea," Melanie chimed in enthusiastically. "How cool would that be? Ashleigh riding Wonder's colt!"

"Well, I—" Christina opened and closed her mouth

in confusion. *Why not?* she asked herself. *Mom's one of the greatest jockeys of all time. I should be thrilled.*

Frowning, Christina watched her mother as she chattered on about riding Star. Her cheeks were pink with excitement. Christina hadn't seen her mother so animated since before Wonder died.

So why was she balking at the idea?

It's only for one race, Christina told herself.

Besides, her mother was way better than George or some other jockey Brad might choose.

Ashleigh was looking at Christina, as if waiting for her approval. Christina rubbed Star's neck. "Okay," she agreed reluctantly. "I think it's a good idea, too."

Ashleigh smiled in relief and turned to Brad. "Is that all right with you?" she asked.

Brad threw open his arms in a gesture of surrender. "Do I have a choice?"

"Good. I'll start exercising him tomorrow," Ashleigh said. "I've got almost two full weeks before his race." She massaged the white star on Star's forehead. "That should be enough for us to get to know each other, right, handsome?"

"You mean you're going to ride him every day?" Christina asked, a hollow feeling growing in her stomach.

"Not every day. You can still ride him once in a while."

Christina gulped. *Once in a while?*

"You sure you're all right?" Ashleigh asked Melanie once more.

"Fine. I must be made out of rubber," Melanie answered with a laugh. "Don't worry about me. Chris will help me put him up."

"Thanks, Mel," Ashleigh said, and hurried after Brad and Mike, who had started toward the gap. As they walked away Christina could hear snatches of their conversation. Ashleigh was talking about Star, her voice high with excitement.

Christina didn't know how she felt, but *excited* wasn't the right word. Raising his head, Star bumped her cheek with his nose as if to say, *What's next?*

Christina glanced at Melanie. "Are you *sure* you're okay?" she repeated. Melanie had been so silent, Christina knew something was wrong.

Looking down, Melanie scuffed her boot in the soft dirt. "Yeah. It's just the first time I've fallen in a while. It kind of scared me."

Christina touched her cousin's shoulder. "It would be weirder if it didn't scare you." She handed Star's reins back to her cousin. "And I know just what you need to do now."

Melanie took the reins. "What?"

"Get back on and take him once around at an easy canter."

"Right," Melanie muttered as she strapped on her helmet. "Tell *him* that."

Christina laughed as she boosted her cousin into the saddle. Again Star gave her a confused look. She knew why Star was giving Melanie so much trouble. He still didn't completely trust anyone else.

As the two trotted away Christina wished with all her heart that she were the one on Star's back. Suddenly she realized why she was so hesitant about her mother riding Star. As bad as it sounded, she was afraid Ashleigh and Star would get along.

All her life Christina had been envious of the bond her mother had had with Wonder. Now Christina had the same sort of bond with Star, and she didn't want to give him up.

"I'm going to race claimers," Christina told her mom and dad that night at dinner. "Phil's a great trainer. I've talked to his exercise riders and grooms, and they all love working for him. I think he can teach me a lot."

Christina had waited until dessert to ask her parents about riding for Phil. She had chosen her words carefully so it wouldn't slip out that she'd already been riding for him.

Silently Ashleigh and Mike listened to what she had to say. Mike was leaning back in his chair, his arms folded across his chest. Ashleigh had stopped eating the chocolate pudding Christina had made. Even Melanie had put down her spoon and was staring at Christina with rapt attention.

"You'll like Phil, Mom," Christina continued. "His dad is Sterling Oberman. He's been a trainer at the Kentucky tracks for years. Both he and Phil have good reputations. Phil's just starting out. That's the only reason he's not training high-class horses."

Christina paused to take a breath, fully expecting her parents to interrupt. But neither one said anything.

"It's the *only* way I'm going to get enough experience," she persisted. "Phil needs a jockey, and he's willing to give me a try. It's perfect."

Clearing his throat, Mike rested his elbow on the table. Ashleigh was frowning at him. Christina shot Melanie a gloomy look that said, *They didn't buy it,* but Melanie winked back.

"I know Phil," Melanie said enthusiastically. "He does have a *great* reputation. His jockeys always say he's a *great* trainer. I think it's a *great* opportunity for Christina."

Christina flashed her cousin an appreciative smile. She knew by the number of *great*s that Melanie was exaggerating, but she needed all the help she could get.

Ashleigh looked at Mike. "Phil *is* known as a promising trainer."

"I'd rather you stick with Whitebrook horses," Mike grumbled. "You did fine with Pride this weekend, and we have a lot more horses you can ride."

"But that was only one race!" Christina protested. "It's not enough. And it's not as though I'm riding for Phil forever. It's just so I can get more experience. Just until his regular jockey's knee heals."

As Christina gazed pleadingly at her father, Mike's expression began to soften. Christina crossed her fingers under the table. Had she talked him into it?

"Okay. It's fine with me," he said.

"Me too," Ashleigh agreed. "Two weeks ago I was dead set against you riding claimers. I'm not totally for it now, but it will give you invaluable experience."

Christina jumped up and leaned across the table to give her mother a hug, upsetting her glass. "Sorry!" she apologized. Melanie burst into a fit of giggles.

"But before you do, I want to meet Phil and talk to him," Ashleigh said, dabbing at the milk with her napkin.

"Of course," Christina said, standing up to help Melanie and Ashleigh clear the table. "You won't be sorry. It's been such an amazing exp—" She caught herself, horrified at what she'd said. "I mean, it *will be* invaluable experience," she corrected hastily.

Ashleigh's gaze was piercing. Her cheeks on fire, Christina busied herself with rinsing the dishes. Had her mother caught her slip?

"Just be careful," Ashleigh said. "You don't know what sort of horrible things can happen on the track."

Oh, yes I do, Christina thought, thinking about Swept Away. "Don't worry, Mom. I won't do anything foolish. I promise."

"And we won't do anything foolish now that we have our learner's permits, either," Melanie said quickly, as if she knew Christina needed rescuing. They had picked up their learner's permits that afternoon.

"Well, neither of you can drive until you've taken the driver's ed course, anyway." Ashleigh said. "I want you to be prepared."

Melanie and Christina groaned, but Christina knew better than to argue. Not only did her mother have that I'm-not-going-to-change-my-mind look on her face, but Christina had already gotten what she really wanted—permission to ride for Phil.

After helping her mom clean up, Christina and Melanie went upstairs. Melanie followed Christina into her bedroom.

"So that's what you've been hiding from me!" Melanie exclaimed, shutting the door behind her as soon as they were in the room. "You weren't at a clinic last week. You were riding for Phil Oberman!"

"Was my slip that obvious?" Going over to her dresser, Christina pulled out a T-shirt.

"I don't think your mom caught it." Melanie

107

dropped down on Christina's bed. "You were pretty convincing."

"And don't you breathe a word about it to anyone," Christina warned Melanie. "Parker is the only other person who knows. Don't even tell Kevin. If it gets back to my parents that I was lying last week, they'll . . . they'll . . ." She couldn't think of anything bad enough.

"Kill you?" Melanie guessed.

"Worse." Clutching the shirt, Christina sat on the edge of the bed and told Melanie about the races she'd been in, excited to finally share her stories about Cat City and Swept Away.

"Cool. Are you riding anyone in two weeks? That's when Susan and my dad are here."

"Well, they'll get to see my mom riding Star," Christina said. "Hey, have you told your dad yet how much you've been racing?"

"No, but I think he'll get the picture when he comes. I'll be riding all day Saturday. The Owenses are putting me on a filly named Sugarplum and a colt named Hero. Plus your parents are putting me on Dazzle and Fast Gun, and—"

"Fast Gun?" Christina interrupted. "The colt that keeps trying to eat people?"

"I'll be on his back," Melanie said. "So he won't get the chance. Besides, Dani's doing a good job with him. He's settled down a little."

108

As Melanie and Christina chattered on about the upcoming races, a heavy tiredness stole over Christina. Her arms felt numb, and she could barely keep her eyes open. But it was a good tiredness, and the weight of lying to her parents had finally been lifted.

Now I won't have to sneak around, Christina thought as she fell back on her bed. Melanie scooted over, and Christina tucked a pillow under her head. Instantly her eyes closed and she fell fast asleep.

Christina propped her arms on the track railing, watching her mother canter Star around the oval. It was early Wednesday morning, the second time Ashleigh had ridden Star. The colt's chestnut coat gleamed, and his thick tail streamed behind him.

Leaning slightly forward in the saddle, Ashleigh swayed rhythmically with the colt's stride. The two moved so smoothly, they seemed to float. Her mother's cheeks were flushed, and when Star breezed past, an elated smile lit up Ashleigh's face.

They went great together.

Christina bit back her feelings of jealousy. Her mother had scrapbooks filled with articles and mementos about Wonder and all her wins. Christina had wanted her own scrapbook filled with stories about Star. But now her mother was replacing her.

"A penny for your thoughts."

Christina swung around. Parker was striding up the path to the track.

"How about if I give *you* a penny if you can guess what I'm thinking about?" Christina said.

Coming up beside her, Parker leaned on the railing, too. "That's easy," he said after watching Ashleigh and Star for a few minutes. The pair had slowed to a trot. Star's neck was arched, and his stride was so full of energy, he looked as though he were dancing. "You're thinking about how well they're doing together and that they'll probably win the Debutante Stakes."

Digging in her jeans pocket, Christina pulled out a penny and plunked it in Parker's outstretched hand. "You won."

"You don't sound too happy," Parker said. "And I don't mean about losing the penny."

"I'm happy my mom's riding him," Christina declared. "I am. I just wish *I* were riding him, that's all."

"Then why aren't you?"

"Because Star deserves a winning jockey, which I am not."

Parker chuckled. "You're the only one who thinks that."

"Maybe," Christina answered, frowning. *But it's true*, she added silently.

"So," Parker added, hastily changing the subject,

"can I count on you to cheer me on this Saturday at the Lexington Park event, or will you be racing those crazy claimers?"

"Sure. I'm only riding for Phil on Thursday and Friday, and my parents don't have anyone for me to ride, so Saturday's all yours."

"Hey, you two," Ashleigh called as she rode up on Star. "How did we look?"

Christina walked over to Star's head and scratched under his mane. "You look great together. I think he really likes you," she said honestly. Star snorted noisily and thrust his nose into Christina's chest.

"He was such a dream!" Ashleigh exclaimed as she dismounted. "I felt like he was really listening to me." Pulling off her helmet, she ran her fingers through her tousled hair. Her cheeks were flushed and her eyes sparkled.

"Dad keeps going on about what a tough race the Debutante is going to be," Parker commented.

"Oh, I'm not worried," Ashleigh said with a laugh. "I don't dare go to the track after being away for so long and make a fool of myself in front of thousands of people."

"I'll bathe him and cool him off, Mom," Christina said, looping the reins over Star's head.

Ashleigh shook her head, taking the reins from Christina. "I want to do it, Chris," she insisted. "I need

111

Star to get to know and trust me. Besides, weren't you going to the track to gallop horses for Phil?"

"Uh, yeah," Christina mumbled.

"Well, I'd better head out of here," Parker said. "Sam has me teaching a lesson at eight. I'll call you tonight, Chris," he added, and jogged off.

Ashleigh clucked to Star. "Come on, handsome. Let's have a nice warm bath."

"Can't I at least help you?" Christina asked, walking alongside them.

"No, thanks. You head on over to Ellis Park."

"Are you sure?" Christina asked, stopping in her tracks.

"Positive," her mother called over her shoulder as she led Star away.

Christina stood rooted to the spot, feeling helpless and alone as they disappeared into the barn.

10

It was Saturday, the day of Parker's event. That morning Parker and Christina had followed the van from Whisperwood to Lexington Park. When Parker and Tor lowered the ramp she was surprised to see Sterling Dream.

"Surprise," Parker announced. "Look who I'm riding at the preliminary level!"

"Kaitlin wasn't ready yet," Tor explained. "But Sterling's definitely ready, and Foxy could use a rest. So Kaitlin agreed to let Parker try her out."

Sterling looked so gorgeous, Christina had to bite her lip to keep from crying. "Hey, sweetheart. I've missed you," she said, stroking the mare's soft muzzle. Eager to be unloaded, Sterling struck the wooden floor with her front hoof.

113

"Kaitlin and Parker must be taking really good care of you," Christina said as she smoothed the mare's silky gray forelock. Her dapples shone like polished nickels, and her mane had been expertly pulled and combed. Red wraps protected her legs, and her halter had a brass name tag on it.

"Go ahead and unload her," Parker called up the ramp. After unhooking the crossties, Christina led Sterling down the ramp. Halfway down the mare leaped to the ground, almost pulling Christina off her feet. "I'd forgotten how excited she gets at these things!" she gasped, laughing.

"You used to get pretty excited, too," Samantha teased. Kevin's half sister had the same red hair and freckles he did. Samantha had brought Sweet Dreams, a filly she'd been working with for several years, to the event to show in the pre-training level. Wistfully Christina thought back to her own dreams of being on the Olympic combined training team. When Star was born, her dreams had shifted. And once she started racing him, she'd given up eventing altogether.

Christina led Sterling around, letting the mare sniff and snort at the strange sights and smells. Christina waved at some people she recognized from her eventing days, and they waved back

She led Sterling away from the vans and trailers toward the edge of the cross-country course and let the mare graze while she looked out across the rolling hills. Lexington Park had tricky jumps designed to blend with the landscape. There were brushes, banks, rock piles, and coops. Christina smiled. It was such a fun course to ride. The bank was especially difficult, since it was built into the side of a steep hill. She would need to slow Sterling to a trot—

"Chris!" Parker called her name, interrupting Christina's thoughts. Turning, she saw him striding down the hill toward them, and her smile faded. She'd almost forgotten that Parker was riding Sterling in the event, not her.

Had she made a huge mistake selling Sterling and giving all this up?

No, I have Star now, Christina reminded herself. *If only I could ride him.*

Sunday morning Christina woke early and dragged herself out of bed. Parker and Sterling had won their event, and Christina had stayed late at Whisperwood celebrating. But this morning she wanted to see Star. Since it was Sunday, the horses in training had the day off. That meant Christina could visit the colt without her mother around.

She threw on jeans and a T-shirt, grabbed an apple, and walked up to the training barn. Ian was leading

Star outside to his turnout for his early morning romp before it got too hot.

Christina followed them out to the paddock, and for a minute she and Ian hung over the fence rail, watching the handsome colt prance from one end of the paddock to the other. His coat looked like shiny copper in the morning sun; his muscles rippled with each step.

Christina munched on her apple, content just to watch him.

Ian finally broke the silence. "I'm worried about your colt."

"Worried?" Christina stopped in midbite. "About what? Every time I watch my mom ride him, he looks great."

Ian bobbed his head in agreement. "Looks great. But he runs slow. I clocked him yesterday without your mom knowing, and his time's way off. I'm not sure what's wrong." Rubbing his jaw, Ian thought a minute. "I want to clock you on him this morning. Later, when your mom and dad go into town."

"But—" Christina started to protest. Ian's expression was so solemn, though, that she realized he must be seriously worried—worried enough to go behind her parents' backs.

"Okay," she agreed. "I'll hang around."

Ian nodded mysteriously, then went back to the barn. Christina didn't follow him. Her heart was beating too

116

fast. Why were Star's times so bad? she wondered. But that wasn't what was making her heart thump. She was going to ride Star again—she couldn't wait!

"He feels great," Christina told Ian an hour later as she trotted Star clockwise up the track. He was alert and soft, and his feet seemed to glide over the smooth dirt track.

"He looks great, too," Ian called. "Let's see what happens when I clock him. Breeze him from the three-quarters pole to the wire."

Christina nodded. Before she even touched him with her heels, Star broke into rolling canter. *It's as if he read my mind*, Christina thought, grinning.

She cantered past the three-quarters pole, then trotted to the rail and turned the colt counterclockwise. The track stretched before them, empty and serene.

"It's just you and me, Star," Christina whispered, her adrenaline pumping. When they passed the pole, she hunkered over his neck and pushed her hands forward. "Go!"

Star burst into a gallop, his long legs snatching at the track as he thundered on. Cool morning air buffeted Christina's cheeks, and the thud of Star's hooves matched the rhythm of her heart. They were one, flying like the wind.

When they galloped past the quarter pole, Christina stayed low on Star's neck. "Go, go, go," she whispered, her words keeping time with his every stride. When they blew past the wire, Christina didn't want to stop. She wanted to keep galloping forever.

But then she heard Ian whoop, and the sound brought her back to reality. Standing in her stirrups, she eased Star to a canter. The colt shook his head, just as reluctant to stop as Christina.

She slowed the colt to a trot and turned him back to where Ian was jogging onto the track.

"Well?" Christina asked breathlessly.

Ian's grin stretched from ear to ear. "He just broke every Whitebrook record I know!"

"I knew it!" Christina exclaimed. She flopped down on Star's neck, letting her arms hang, and laid her palms on his shoulders. "Feel him! He barely broke a sweat!"

"I wish I knew why he wasn't going this fast for your mother," Ian said. "With the times they've been putting in, he'll come in dead last."

Instantly Christina's excitement dimmed. "They still have one more week before the race. Maybe his works will be faster when we take him to the track on Thursday."

Ian shook his head. "Let's hope so. Star needs that win this weekend. Otherwise Brad's gonna be breathing down our necks even worse."

Sliding off Star, Christina faced Ian. "Ian, we can't tell Mom about Star's time today. Right?"

"No way. Ashleigh's having too much fun. I don't want to ruin it for her."

Ian left her to cool Star off. As she walked the colt around the track Christina thought about what the trainer had said. This past week her mother had been in a great mood. Not only had she declared that riding Star felt almost as wonderful as riding Wonder again, she was sure they were going to win the next weekend.

Christina didn't want to ruin it for Ashleigh, either.

Christina paced outside Star's stall at Ellis Park, worrying her bottom lip with her top teeth. It was late Saturday morning, the day of Star's race, and nothing was going right.

Wednesday evening they'd brought Star to Ellis Park. Thursday morning his works had been dismal. The official clocker had timed him at a lazy 1:59:40 for the mile. At first Ian and Christina didn't know what to think. They'd checked his temperature. His legs. His wind. Everything was fine.

Ashleigh had shrugged off Star's poor time. "We'll do fine in the race" was all she'd said, her tone confident. Christina hoped her mother was right, but she was beginning to have her doubts.

Christina stopped her pacing to listen. She could hear Brad's voice thundering from the spare stall White-brook was using as an office and storeroom.

"Did you see the *Racing Form*?" he was shouting. "Do you see who Star's up against? Dangerous and Jupiter's Moon. No way can he beat them with the times he's been putting in. Unless you want to be laughed off the track, we should scratch him from this race!"

Plugging her ears, Christina fled into Star's stall. He whinnied happily, oblivious to the storm breaking around him.

"I'm glad you're not nervous," she told him. "You're just about the only one who is keeping cool." *Too cool,* Christina decided.

The sound of footsteps drew Christina toward the open top of the stall door. Hidden in the shadows, she peeked outside. Brad was striding from the barn, his shoulders rigid. Ian and Mike were standing in the doorway, watching him go. It was clear they had not backed down. The two men ducked back into the office.

"I'll be right back," Christina whispered to Star. Opening the stall door, she ran into the office. Mike and Ian instantly stopped talking.

Christina's brows shot up. "What's wrong?"

Ian immediately began busying himself with some papers on the desk.

Mike massaged his temples as if he had a headache.

120

"We just spent the last fifteen minutes reassuring Brad that Star would not disgrace Townsend Acres. The thing is, we probably should scratch him. Star's not running well. But we can't figure out what's wrong."

"Star's fine," Christina said, glancing at Ian. Should they tell Mike about his incredible time on Sunday?

"You seem to be the only one convinced of that," Mike said.

"Mom's still confident he can win."

"Yes, but running on Whitebrook's track isn't the same as running a race," Ian said. "Star's been acting like he's on a vacation."

"He'll run well. I know he will," Christina declared. She hurried away before her father could see how worried she really was.

Ashleigh was walking toward her down the lane between the two barns, followed by a group of reporters and cameramen. Ever since Ashleigh had arrived that morning, they'd been dogging her every step.

"So far Star's shown speed in only one race," one of the reporters said loudly. "Do you really think he has Wonder's ability to win the Kentucky Derby?"

"Absolutely," Ashleigh said, her tone sure. "He's a colt, so it's taking him longer to mature. Give him time, and he may even do better than Wonder."

"When he does make it to the big leagues, will you

be riding him, Ashleigh?" another reporter asked.

Ashleigh shook her head and laughed, obviously enjoying the spotlight. "Who knows?" she said. "First we have to get there."

Christina looked on silently. *We?*

"Here she is, folks!" the announcer called over the loud-speaker. "Ashleigh Griffen, winning jockey of the Triple Crown, back on the track after a twelve year hiatus! Let's give her a standing ovation!"

Christina leaned her arms on the railing in front of the grandstand. Behind her, the crowd roared and applauded. Out on the track in the post parade, Ashleigh waved happily to the appreciative crowd, and Star plodded toward the starting gate like an obedient trail horse. Christina had helped get the colt ready for the race, talking to him and trying to psych him up. But when she'd handed him off to the pony rider, she knew she'd have to face facts—the outcome of the race was up to Star and Ashleigh.

When the noise died down, the announcer continued. "Ashleigh won the Kentucky Derby and the Belmont on Ashleigh's Wonder, bred and trained at Townsend Acres, and the Triple Crown on her colt, Wonder's Champion. Today she's riding another one of Wonder's colts, Wonder's Star, who is jointly owned and trained by Whitebrook Farm and Townsend Acres. The two farms have high hopes for this colt, and the world will be watching to see if he'll follow in his dam's hoofprints!"

Christina grimaced. She couldn't believe Star and her mom were getting so much attention. Talk about pressure!

She glanced into the grandstand and could just make out Brad, Lavinia, and their friends in the Townsends' private box. If Star ran badly and the media plastered the news on every sports page, Brad would be so furious he might even take Star away again.

Just then Parker came through the crowd carrying two sodas. The summer sun was beating down on the onlookers, and sweat rolled off Christina's temples.

"Wow, that was quite a sendoff," Parker commented, searching Christina's face worriedly. When she didn't say anything, he added, "How's Star look?"

"Like an old plow horse," Christina grumbled. She took a sip of her soda, savoring the cool drink. Parker had his binoculars draped around his neck. Raising them, he peered down the track toward the starting gate. "He doesn't look so bad."

"Let me see." Christina leaned close to Parker and gazed through the binoculars, trying to locate Star. He was number seven, a terrible position in a field of eight. But at least he didn't have to wait in the gate for very long while the other horses loaded.

Finally Christina found him. Ashleigh was circling him far back from the other horses. Christina could see her squeezing him with her heels. The colt's ears flicked back and forth, but at least he was becoming more animated.

Star loaded easily. When the eighth horse walked in, Christina held her breath. *This is it.*

Seconds later the front gates burst open and the horses leaped onto the track. Christina dropped the binoculars. As the field swept toward her it seemed as if all eight horses were running neck and neck in a straight line.

Then slowly the pack shifted as a few horses dropped back and others moved toward the rail. Christina strained to locate Ashleigh's blue-and-white silks.

"And it's Jupiter's Moon in the lead, Freeway second, with Holiday Time third. Wonder's Star, with Ashleigh Griffen on board, is seventh. We'll soon see if the last foal of the famous Ashleigh's Wonder has his dam's speed and stamina."

As the horses blew past, Christina caught sight of Star. He had his ears back. Ashleigh was pumping with her hands, trying to get him to speed up, but the colt's gallop was listless.

"Talk to him, Mom," Christina whispered. "Tell him to win for me."

Taking her hand, Parker held it tightly. "It'll be okay," he said, but Christina could hear the tension in his voice.

"Around the bend, Jupiter's Moon is still in first place. Freeway has dropped back. Dangerous is gaining. Holiday Time is fighting for second. Wonder's Star is still seventh. Ashleigh is giving the colt a super ride. She hasn't lost her form. But does she have the touch? And does the colt have the talent?"

Yes, he does! Christina gritted her teeth. Why was the stupid announcer focusing so much on Star? "Boy, would I love to shove that microphone up the announcer's nose," she grumbled to Parker.

He laughed. "Hey, you're always talking about your special connection with Star. Why don't you use it? Send him some vibes. Tell him to get his lazy butt moving!"

This time Christina had to laugh. But then she thought, *Why not? It's worth a try.*

Closing her eyes, she concentrated hard. She pictured herself breezing Star. She felt the wind against her face, the thud of his hooves, the power of his stride, his will to win.

"Go, Star. Run for me," she whispered, squeezing her eyes shut.

Beside her, Parker gasped, then nudged Christina. "Look at that!"

Christina opened her eyes. The horses were coming around the final bend. She could just make out Star on the outside of the tightly clumped field.

And he was gaining fast.

"Wonder's Star is making an incredible run from behind!" the announcer hollered. "He's in third place and closing. Ashleigh Griffen is driving him on with everything she's got."

As Star flew down the track toward the finish line, Christina jumped up and down, screaming with excitement. Parker pumped his fist in the air. "Go! Go!" they both shouted.

"Wonder's Star easily overtakes Jupiter's Moon, who's flagging. Now it's a battle between Dangerous and Wonder's Star. Another incredible burst of speed, and Wonder's Star wins by a nose. What a race from behind! What a terrific team—Ashleigh Griffen and Wonder's Star!"

Christina threw her arms around Parker. He picked her up and swung her around, whooping with happiness.

"He did it!" Christina gasped, eyes glimmering with tears of joy.

Parker took her hand. "Let's meet them at the winner's circle."

By the time they got there, the crowd surrounding Ashleigh and Star was thick.

"What a great story!" a reporter hollered to Ashleigh as she weighed herself. "Ashleigh Griffen, winning jockey, does it again on Ashleigh's Wonder's colt."

"His name is Wonder's Star," Ashleigh told the reporter. "And don't you forget it!"

Cameras snapped and flashed and reporters yelled out questions. Even the clerk of scales beamed at Ashleigh as if it was the first win he'd ever witnessed.

"Wonder's Star easily beat Jupiter's Moon and Dangerous, two up-and-coming three-year-olds, in the Debutante Stakes, a tough race," another reporter said. "That was quite a feat. Are you prepping him for next year's Triple Crown?"

"Hey," Parker murmured to Christina. "Judging from the reaction of the reporters, you'd think Star had just won the Kentucky Derby."

"Come on. I want to see Star." Taking Parker's hand, Christina tried to push through the crowd. A journalist shoved in front of her, his video camera banging her in the head. A girl with a WE LOVE ASHLEIGH poster ran into her, almost knocking her over. By the time Christina reached the edge of the winner's circle, the photos were being taken. Christina halted behind an official whose arms were outstretched, barring the way.

Her gaze flew to Star, who was posing proudly. Mike had one hand lightly on the bridle. Brad and Lavinia held the trophy between them. And Ashleigh beamed down from the saddle.

"Yup, I knew the colt could do it," Brad was saying to the onlookers as if it had been his idea to enter Star in the mile. "The whole time we were training him at Townsend Acres, I figured he was going to be my next champion."

Christina rolled her eyes.

"That's my dad!" Parker said with mock pride.

"Ashleigh! An interview!" a persistent reporter called. Her mother dismounted. Pushing past the official, Christina ran up and took Star's reins from Mike. "I'll take him," she whispered to her dad. "You stay with Mom while she basks in her glory."

"What about you? You deserve a little basking."

Christina shook her head. "I just want to be with Star."

Looking over her shoulder, she flashed Parker a smile, then mouthed, "See you later."

He nodded as if he understood she needed some time alone. Quickly she led Star away from the milling crowd, breathing a sigh of relief when she reached the quiet of the test barn, where Star would be checked by a vet for drugs.

There she finally gave him the hug he deserved. "You're the best," she told Star as he blew softly against her cheek. "You're going to show them all."

After the vet gave Star a clean bill, Christina took

him back to the barn, untacked him, and started on his bath.

When she turned the warm water on him, Star danced and kicked at the spray. Christina laughed, glad to see him acting like a silly colt instead of a proud champion.

Several people came up and congratulated her on the horse's win. Christina thanked them, feeling oddly hollow inside. What would happen now? Would Brad insist that her mother ride Star in all his races? Would Mike and Ashleigh agree?

After all, the reporters and announcers had called Star and Ashleigh a winning team. And wasn't that the most important thing?

Taking the sponge, Christina gently wiped Star's face. "Maybe I'm not the best jockey for you," she whispered to the colt. "The most important thing is that you become a champion. Even if I never ride you again."

At the thought, Christina's heart grew tight with sadness. She ducked her head, sloshing the sponge in the bucket, trying to keep busy so she wouldn't cry.

"There's the winner," she heard someone say. It was her mother's voice.

Before she raised her head, Christina took a deep breath. She didn't want her mother to see how upset she was. This was Ashleigh's moment of triumph.

"Does he *still* look like a champion?" Christina said with false lightness, pointing to the soapsuds dotting the colt's cheeks. Star shook his head, spraying them, and Ashleigh laughed.

"Maybe the reporters wouldn't think so," Ashleigh said with a smile. She slipped an arm around Christina's shoulder. "Thank you for letting me ride him today," she told her daughter. "It was very special."

"No, thank *you!*" Christina blurted. "Star needed that win. He was beginning to get discouraged. Now you and Star can get ready for the Magnolia Stakes," Christina rushed on. "I've already looked into the race. It's in two weeks. He should be ready by then."

Ashleigh held up her hand. "Wait a minute," she said. "What do you mean, me and Star? I only planned to ride Star in this one race. You're his jockey."

Christina turned away, picking up the hose to spray the soap off Star's side. She didn't want her mother to see her face. "No. You're the best jockey for Star," she said, trying to keep the tremor out of her voice.

"Me?" Ashleigh demanded. She put her hand on Christina's shoulder and turned Christina around. "Oh, Chris, how can you say that? Star didn't win today because of me. He won because *he* chose to win."

"What do you mean? You heard the reporters. They said you were a terrific team."

Ashleigh shook her head. "They don't know what

130

they're talking about. I know how it feels to be in sync with a horse. I had it with Wonder. When we raced together, it was magic. Star and I don't have that magic. But you two do. You have what it takes to win."

Christina furrowed her brows. "Did Ian tell you about our fast time on Sunday?" she asked suspiciously.

"No. He didn't have to. I've seen you ride Star," Ashleigh explained. "I've seen how you communicate with each other. If Star becomes a champion, it will be because you—and only you—are riding him."

"Oh, Mom." Christina couldn't keep the tears back any longer. She threw her arms around her mother and cried into her blue-and-white silks.

"You've worked hard these past few weeks, Christina Reese," Ashleigh said in her ear, her voice tight. "Phil told me he couldn't have asked for a more professional jock for his string. And I couldn't be prouder. You *deserve* to ride Star in his next race."

"But what about Brad?" Christina choked out. "He won't like it."

"I'll take care of him," Ashleigh promised.

"Thanks." Christina pulled back and smiled at her mother. "But in the meantime I want to keep riding the other horses. I need all the experience I can get before Star's race."

"Good. Next weekend you can ride Rhapsody for Whitebrook," Ashleigh said. "She's entered in the Ellis

Allowance. It's a big purse and should attract some good fillies. If you do well on her, maybe other trainers will be interested in letting you ride for them."

"And Phil wants me to ride some more horses for him, too," Christina added excitedly. "By the time Star races again, I should be ready!" Pulling away from her mom, she gave Star a big hug.

Suddenly something cold and wet splattered against the nape of Christina's neck. She jumped back. Star had picked up the sponge and was waving it in the air.

"Hey!" She reached for it, and he ran backward, knocking over the bucket of soapy water. Ashleigh danced in the spill, trying to keep her feet dry. Then Star dropped the sponge and lifted his upper lip in a silly face.

"If only the reporters could see him now," Christina said, laughing. "The headlines would say, 'Wonder's Star, the Clown of Whitebrook Farm, Wins the Debutante!'"

11

NOW THAT CHRISTINA WAS RIDING STAR AGAIN, SHE WAS busier than ever. The colt had Sunday and Monday off, then a light workout Tuesday and Wednesday. Thursday morning Christina headed to Ellis Park. She was riding a new colt Phil was training, named Favorite Game, in the third race that day. She'd breezed him Tuesday for his work, and Phil was pleased with his time. But Fave, as he was nicknamed, was gangly and silly, and on the mornings she exercised him she'd worn herself out trying to keep him running in a straight line.

When Christina came into the jockey room to get ready for the race, she spotted Sammy and George sitting on the worn sofa watching TV. Christina was surprised to see George. He hadn't been around for the past two weeks.

"I come back and there's the *same* bug problem," George said to Sammy after glancing at Christina. "I thought maybe the exterminator had been here."

Ignoring him, Christina went into the locker room. Vicky Frontiere was changing into her silks. She must have noticed the glum look on Christina's face, since she asked, "What's wrong?"

"George and Sammy are what's wrong. I try to ignore them, but they still get to me."

"Those two are like the bullies on the school playground," Vicky said. "And for some reason they've decided to pick on you."

"I don't see why. I've never bothered them. Where's George been, anyway? Not that I've missed him."

"He was suspended for two weeks."

Christina cocked her head. "What for?"

"Whipping his horse after a race. Angelo, one of the outriders, caught him smacking the colt because it hadn't won. Angelo told George to get off the horse. George did, but when he strode off, he started yelling at Angelo." Vicky shook her head. "Major mistake. Angelo's been around forever, and he doesn't tolerate disrespect. The stewards suspended George, and now that he's back, he's not allowed to use a whip. They also said the next time he pulled anything like that, they'd kick him off the Kentucky tracks for good."

"If they do, I won't miss him." Christina dropped down on the bench to pull off her sneakers. She was glad the stewards had taken the whip away from George. He wouldn't be able to pull another stunt like the one he'd pulled on Star.

"I don't think any of the jockeys would miss him." Vicky picked up her goggles and helmet. "He hasn't won much lately, and it's made him nasty." She waved as she was leaving. "See you in the third race."

"You're riding in that race, too?"

"Yup. A colt named Forever Fast." She chuckled. "Except he should have been named Forever Slow. I usually don't ride on Thursdays, but I'm riding him for a friend, who won't take my advice and sell him to someone for a backyard pet. He keeps thinking the colt will one day turn into a speed demon. In the meantime, he's losing money—fast."

Christina laughed. When Vicky left, the locker room seemed quiet and empty even though several other women jockeys were changing. She was relieved to hear that Vicky was in her race. At least one jockey would be riding clean and fair.

She changed into green-and-gold silks—Phil's colors. Pulling out a can of black polish and an old sock, Christina cleaned up her leather boots. She wanted to stay in the locker room until it was time to go to the viewing paddock. Okay, so she was a chicken. But she didn't feel like listening to George's and Sammy's nasty comments.

When it was time to go, she walked into the main room. George was leaving with the group of jockeys riding in the third race. Christina's heart sank. She couldn't believe her bad luck.

You can't let him get to you, she admonished herself. There would always be jockeys like George, and she'd have to learn to deal with them. Catching up to Vicky, she walked with her out the door.

Before they got to the paddock, George turned and pointed his finger at her. "Stay out of my way, bug. I may not have a whip, but that won't stop me from winning."

Bristling, Christina returned his icy stare. Vicky touched her on the shoulder. "Save that energy for the race," she told Christina. "Don't waste it on him."

Christina took a deep breath. "You're right."

Phil was waiting at the paddock with Favorite Game. Fave was twirling around, staring excitedly at the other horses and riders. When Christina came up, he nipped at her helmet, ripping off the green-and-gold cover.

"Hey!" She reached for it, but he raised his head, flapping it in the air. The movement startled the colt behind him, who reared and stumbled into the horse beside him. Grooms, trainers, and jockeys hollered.

Christina flushed. This was not a good start.

Phil steadied the colt, and when Fave dropped his nose, he grabbed the helmet cover out of his mouth. "Better hang on to this," he said, passing it to Christina. "Come on, let's get you in the saddle, where you'll be safe."

Taking the cover, Christina followed Phil to the saddling stall. Fave bounced inside, then began to paw at the dirt.

"He's like a big puppy—so full of himself," Christina said to Phil as she replaced the cover. "I just hope I can get him going in a straight line so he can use that energy getting to the wire."

Phil chuckled as he put the number blanket on the colt's back. "You must have read my mind. That was going to be my one and only instruction: Keep him moving in a straight line."

Christina handed Phil the saddle. He hoisted it onto the colt's back and began to tighten the girth. With a squeal, Fave hopped in the air and kicked sideways. Christina jumped out of the way.

"I think I *will* be safer on him than down here!" she exclaimed with a laugh.

"Stay with the pony rider until you're inside the starting gate," Phil advised after the paddock judge called for the riders to mount up. "Otherwise you'll wear yourself out before the race." He boosted her into the saddle.

"And don't forget he's still goofy at the start."

Fave was quivering all over with excitement. Christina could feel the power and eagerness in the colt's stride. As Phil led Fave to the gate, she grinned down at the trainer. "I have a good feeling about this guy," she said. "If nobody claims him, he may be good enough to move to the big races, and you'll be training your first allowance horse!"

Phil forced back a smile. "I'm not even going to think about it," he said. "I don't want to jinx the race."

"Christina!" A familiar voice made her look over to the railing around the paddock. Ashleigh and Melanie were waving enthusiastically.

"You go, girl!" Melanie called.

"Good luck, honey!" Ashleigh said.

Christina grinned and waved back. After handing Fave to the pony rider, Phil wished Christina good luck, too.

Favorite Game had drawn number two, a good spot in the field of nine colts. As they cantered next to the pony rider Fave felt strong and eager, and Christina felt a surge of confidence.

In a little over a week I'll be riding Star to the starting gate! Christina thought excitedly.

When they reached the gate, Fave balked, refusing to enter the narrow chute. Finally he jumped forward, banging Christina's foot against the metal side as he scrambled into the stall. It was a long wait until the last horse was loaded, and Christina could feel the colt growing more and more nervous. In the stall next to them, Vicky gave Christina a thumbs-up sign. "George's number nine," she called over the slam of gates. "He'll be too far away to mess with you."

Christina flashed her a grin of thanks, then the starter yelled, "Last to load," and Christina's heart began to thump wildly.

"And they're off!" the announcer yelled.

Favorite Game charged awkwardly from the gate, stumbling over his own feet. But Christina had anticipated a rocky start, so she was prepared. She kept a firm hold on the reins and pressed him on, trying to keep the colt's confidence up, since by then they were in the back of the field, running with the other bad starters.

But Christina wasn't worried. Fave was a strong colt with a lot of speed. If she could keep him in a straight line and find the right holes, she could move up quickly.

Out of the corner of her eye she spotted George on her right. He was galloping next to her on a whippet-thin chestnut colt. When he drew closer, she could see the nasty sneer on his face.

Before she could react, George had steered his colt so close that their stirrups touched. Then his hand whipped out, and he caught her right rein and gave it a tug—only for a second, but long enough to pull the young horse off balance.

Fave rammed into George's colt, throwing them both off stride. "Get away from my horse!" George hollered furiously.

When she realized what George had done, Christina couldn't believe it. He had forced Fave to bump his horse, and had acted as if it was her fault!

A surge of anger filled Christina. She wasn't going to let George get away with it twice. Teeth clenched, she steered Fave toward George's mount. Two could play bumper cars. Then suddenly she caught herself.

What was she doing? George *wanted* her to go after him. He wanted her to stoop to his level.

She wasn't going to play his game. Tightening her left rein and using her right heel, Christina moved Fave away from George's colt. She spotted a hole between the two horses in front and to her left. Using her body and voice, she urged Fave to go for it. The colt had regained his balance and was only too happy to oblige. With powerful strides he passed between the two colts. When she knew George was well behind her, Christina breathed a sigh of relief.

Just ahead of them, Vicky was in third place on Forever Fast. Out on the rail, two other colts were battling it out for first place. As they neared the fourth furlong Christina could see that Vicky was using all the tricks she had to keep Forever going, but the colt was flagging.

"Got anything left?" Christina hollered up to Vicky. It was the first time she'd ever asked another jockey for help. She knew that if a horse didn't have it in him to win, a courteous jockey like Vicky might make room for a gaining horse.

In response, Vicky reined Forever to the left, leaving room for Fave to surge ahead. Now there was nothing in front but smooth, open track leading to the finish line.

"Go, Fave!" Christina ducked low on the colt's neck. Favorite Game flew past the two horses on the rail, passing under the finish line a length ahead.

"Yes!" Christina exclaimed out loud, and punched her fist into the air. Another win!

Christina slowed Fave to a canter. An outrider wearing a cowboy hat drew alongside them to escort her back to the grandstand. "Nice race," he said, tipping his hat.

"Thanks," Christina said breathlessly. She reached forward to stroke Fave's neck. "Good boy!"

"Fave, you big goof, you did it!" Phil whooped, a huge smile on his face, when they stepped off the track. "You were right about him, Chris." He snapped a lead onto the colt's bridle. Favorite Game butted him hard, then pranced sideways, enjoying the attention.

Christina jumped to the ground, and an attendant whipped off Fave's saddle. Christina planted a kiss on the gangly colt's nose. "You like this winning stuff, huh?"

Quickly Christina hurried to have her weight checked, and then remounted.

Unlike her last win on Star, which was a bigger race, there was only one photographer and no reporters at the winner's circle. Christina tried to keep Fave still while the photographer snapped pictures. Suddenly she heard Phil gasp, "Oh, no."

"What's wrong?" Christina asked, disturbed by his tone of voice.

Phil pointed to the tote board. Favorite Game's number was flashing. So was number nine—George's horse!

A chill swept over Christina. She knew what the flashing numbers meant. George must have made a complaint against her.

Phil glanced up at her. "What happened out there?"

Christina shook her head numbly. "Right after we broke, Fave bumped into the number nine horse. But it wasn't my fault! George rode his horse too close. When the stewards review the films, they'll see that George interfered with *us*."

Phil furrowed his brow as if he wasn't sure who to believe. Christina knew that bugs were usually the cause of mishaps, and Favorite Game had a reputation for zigzagging all over the track. Why would anyone believe her?

She looked back at the tote board, and her heart sank to the ground. Favorite Game had been dropped to dead last and the second-place horse had been declared the winner.

"It looks like the stewards decided it was your fault," Phil said grimly. Then Fave's owners strode up, looking angry, and Phil turned his attention to them.

As Phil led them away, Christina could hear him explaining what had happened. She jumped down from Fave's back and handed the reins to Phil's groom, who took the colt back to the barn.

For a minute Christina stood at the edge of the winner's circle, watching the second-place horse get his photo taken. In five seconds she'd gone from triumphant to crestfallen.

But she knew the bump *hadn't* been her fault, and this time she would fight the complaint.

Fists clenched by her sides, Christina strode away from the winner's circle. Ashleigh and Melanie caught up with her. "What happened?" Ashleigh asked. "You two were great out there. Why were you dropped to last?"

Christina told them what had happened. "It's George again. But he can't get away with this—I'll fight him!"

Melanie scrunched her brows together. "Are you sure you want to, Chris? You're completely positive your colt didn't interfere with George's horse? He looked pretty rambunctious."

"I'm sure," Christina insisted. "Fave stumbled right after we broke from the gate, but he was running smoothly when George purposely grabbed my rein."

"That's a serious accusation," Ashleigh said, frowning. "If you're right, George could get barred from the track."

"It's true, Mom. You've got to believe me."

Ashleigh squeezed Christina's shoulder. "I believe you. I'm just trying to figure out what we can do about it."

"Thanks, but this is my fight." Squaring her shoulders, Christina headed for the jockey room. She went right to the phone, called the stewards, and started to tell the official who answered exactly what had happened. "Thank you, Ms. Reese," the official interrupted her. "We'll review your case and give you a decision tomorrow morning."

Christina felt sick to her stomach. Did that mean they believed George's story? Hot tears pricked her eyes. Quickly she strode into the women's locker room before she saw George.

Christina kicked off her boots in frustration. The next morning, when she was called before the stewards, she would tell them her side of the story, and they'd believe her. They *had* to.

Friday morning Christina reported to the Ellis Park stewards' office. She'd been there several times before to view films or review track rules.

Karen, Fred, and several of the other bugs were sitting around the room watching replays of races. Christina said hi, then perched stiffly on a chair, her eyes glued to the TV monitor.

George came out of one of the offices wearing a gray suit and tie, his hair slicked back as if he was trying to impress someone. As he strode past, he gave Christina a triumphant smile.

Great, Christina thought glumly.

Finally Mr. Lambert, one of the officials, called her into his office.

"Good luck, Chris," Karen called before she went in.

Mr. Lambert was sitting behind a massive mahogany desk. "We've reviewed the film and listened to Mr. Stewart's side of the story, Ms. Reese," he said, eyes grim under bushy gray brows. "And we find no evidence that George interfered with your horse. We've decided to uphold his complaint."

"But you haven't even listened to my side," Christina protested. "George grabbed my horse's rein!"

"As I said, we reviewed the film. Mr. Stewart says that when your horse veered into his, he reached out to push your horse away—which is supported by the footage, I might add. Mr. Stewart claims you had it in for him due to a past incident and that the bump was deliberate. In addition, the colt you were riding has been the subject of several other complaints about interfering with other horses. We have no choice but to stand by our initial ruling."

"But George's story isn't true!" Christina exclaimed, trying to keep the anger out of her voice. "He's the one who had it in for me! Fave did stumble, but it was way before George bumped into *me*. Can't I watch the films with you and point out what really—"

Mr. Lambert raised his hand to silence her. "We have made our ruling. And due to the severity of the charge, we've decided to suspend you for two weeks."

All the color drained from Christina's face. They couldn't suspend her that long. Star's race was only a week away!

12

CHRISTINA OPENED HER MOUTH, READY TO ARGUE, BUT SHE could tell by Mr. Lambert's expression that the stewards had made up their minds. She'd heard stories of jockeys who took the stewards to court to get their suspensions overturned. But those same jockeys had made enemies of the track officials—not a good career move for a young apprentice.

She closed her mouth and stood up. "Thank you," she said quietly, though she had no reason to thank anyone. As she left the room she felt as if she'd been run over by a truck.

When she walked into the foyer, Karen said, "Well?"

Christina shrugged miserably. "Two weeks' suspension."

"Wow!" Everybody's eyes grew large. Bugs were

used to getting suspensions of a day or two for minor infractions, but it was very unusual to get one as long as Christina's.

"That's a lot," Fred exclaimed. "The stewards must have had it in for you."

"You mean George had it in for her," Karen said, shaking her head. "Sorry, Christina."

"Yeah, well, I'll see you guys later—a lot later," she muttered, hurrying from the office before she started crying in front of them.

When Christina left, she wasn't sure what to do. Joe Kisner, the Whitebrook groom who was taking care of the horses at Ellis Park that morning, was supposed to give her a lift home. But that wasn't until lunchtime.

Christina couldn't face the backside. Too many people would ask her questions, plus she didn't want to risk meeting George.

Slowly she made her way to the grandstand. Maybe she could get a soda at the coffee shop. As she dragged herself past the empty betting stalls, Christina felt totally helpless and alone.

"Did you beg and plead with the stewards?" Melanie asked.

Christina nodded miserably. Even though it was

hours later, her head ached and she still felt as if she'd been kicked in the stomach.

Melanie jumped off the overturned bucket and paced across the lawn outside the training barn. The two girls were sitting under a shady tree, cleaning bridles. Christina's parents had gone grocery shopping in preparation for the arrival of Melanie's dad and stepmom that night, so Christina hadn't yet been able to tell them what had happened. Later that afternoon Melanie, Ashleigh, and Mike would be driving to the airport to pick up Will and Susan. Christina hoped she'd be able to talk to her parents before they left.

Tears welled up in Christina's eyes, plopping on the reins she was holding in her lap. After winning the race on Fave, she'd been on top of the world. Now she felt as if she'd sunk to the bottom.

"Why didn't you tell the stewards it was George's fault?" Melanie asked. "That might have at least gotten him suspended, too."

Christina picked up her sponge. "I did," she said, halfheartedly scrubbing a rein. "But in the replay, all you could see was George looking my way. You couldn't see him snatch my rein. It did look like Fave's fault."

Melanie tapped her lip, leaving soapsuds on her cheek. "There's got to be something we can do. You *have* to ride Star in his next race." Suddenly she spun and pointed a finger at Christina. "I've got it! Your parents can list me as Star's jockey. We'll cut your hair and dye it blond. You can take my jockey certificate and ride as me! The clerk of scales won't know the difference."

Christina had been listening with wide eyes, but when Melanie gave her a goofy grin, Christina knew her cousin was only joking around to make her feel better. "Yeah, and we'd both get kicked off the track forever." She exhaled loudly. "It's no use. I won't be able to race Star."

"Hmpf." With a glum look, Melanie sank down on a bucket.

"I can't figure out why George has it in for me," Christina said.

"It's just because you're the newest bug on the track," Melanie explained. Picking up a snaffle bit, she began to polish it. "The journeymen jockeys do it to all of us. It's a ritual. George's just been nastier because of his own bad luck." Melanie waved the bit at Christina. "You know, you're going to have to deal with him sometime," she added, an ominous edge to her words. "Or he's going to keep coming after you."

"Yeah, I guess." Christina pressed her lips together grimly.

When Christina's parents came home from shopping, Christina and Melanie met them at the front door.

"I'll get the rest of the groceries," Melanie offered, hurrying past the three of them and out the door.

Ashleigh must have noticed the worried expression on Christina's face, because she set the bag she was carrying on the hall floor and immediately put an arm around her daughter's shoulder. "Oh, no. Didn't the meeting this morning go well?"

"No." Christina's bottom lip quivered. "I won't be able to race for two weeks!" And she explained what had happened.

"I can't believe they suspended you for two weeks!" Ashleigh exclaimed when Christina had finished. "That's ridiculous! Didn't you explain what happened?"

"I did. But when I watched the replay, it did look as if I was riding recklessly. I guess they had no choice."

"But for two weeks?" Mike repeated, sounding angry. "That's a lot of time to give a bug for bumping a horse."

"George told them I did it deliberately to get back at him for the race I lost on Star."

Crossing her arms, Ashleigh frowned. "That's ridiculous. The stewards know you're my daughter—and they should know you'd never do such a stupid thing!"

"Mom, being your daughter has nothing to do with this."

"Of course it does. The stewards know Whitebrook's reputation. It's impeccable. We've always run a clean operation—in every way. They have no reason to punish you so severely."

151

"I think your mother and I need to talk to the officials," Mike said.

"No!" Christina blurted. "This was my fight, and I lost. Mom, please. I can't stand in your shadow forever."

For a second Ashleigh didn't say anything. Then she gave Christina a faint smile. "I understand," she said softly. "And I'm so sorry about the suspension. I guess you're learning the hard way about the ups and downs of being a jockey."

Christina swallowed the sob rising in her throat. "Any other time I could have handled it. But I've been working so *hard* to get ready for Star's next race. It's not fair!"

"No, it's not," Mike said. Setting down his bags, he wrapped his arms around Christina, and she buried her face in his shirt the way she had when she was little. "But unless you can prove George was the cause of the bump, there's nothing the stewards can do. At least *we* know you're telling the truth."

"Thanks for believing me." Taking a shaky breath, Christina pulled back from her father. "You'll have to get another jockey for Rhapsody for tomorrow's race," she said. "I'm sorry it's such short notice." Stepping away, she wiped the tears off her cheeks. Her mother had tears in her eyes, too. "And Mom, you'll probably have to ride Star in the Magnolia Stakes."

"We'll see," Ashleigh said. "But I don't want you to quit exercise-riding Star." She touched Christina on the shoulder. "Everything will turn out okay, Chris. Don't worry."

As much as she wanted to believe her mother, Christina wasn't so sure.

Saturday evening Christina and Parker made it to the reserved box in time to watch Melanie's last race from the Ellis Park grandstand. They met Will, Susan, Mike, Ashleigh, Ian, and Beth McLean in Whitebrook's private box. Kimberley McFarland, the owner of Fast Gun, the colt Melanie was riding, was there as well.

Kevin, Christina, and Parker had spent the day helping Maureen handle the horses who were racing so that Mike, Ashleigh, Ian, and Beth could enjoy the day with Will and Susan. When they were done, Christina and Parker had rushed home to shower and change while Kevin groomed for Melanie.

Christina had changed into a sundress. After adding a dash of makeup and a pair of sandals, she was ready to try to enjoy the evening. She'd worked so hard all day, she'd barely had time to think about the suspension. She hoped she'd be able to keep it out of her mind that night.

"Mom, Beth, you two look great!" Christina said

after saying hi to everyone. Ashleigh was wearing a black dress and black sandals. Her hair was piled on top of her head, with loose tendrils curling against her cheeks.

Beth McLean, Kevin's mom, was dressed more conservatively in a suit, but she still looked just as nice.

"You look great, too, Susan," Christina added, laughing. "As usual." Melanie's stepmother always looked New York chic—she had an eye for fashion.

"Thanks," Susan said. "I wasn't sure what to wear, but I wanted to be ready for the winner's circle."

"Melanie's on a roll," Christina agreed. "Right, Uncle Will?"

"Did you see her in the last one? Won by three lengths!" Will said proudly. Dressed in a navy sport coat, drink in one hand, binoculars in the other, he fit right in with the racing crowd. He began a blow-by-blow description of Melanie's race on Sugarplum.

Christina laughed. "Very impressive," she said when he'd finished his story. "Have you thought about changing careers? You might make a good race reporter."

"Here they come!" the announcer called. As the horses walked onto the track for the post parade, Christina strained to see over the heads of the crowd in the grandstand and caught a glimpse of Melanie's blue-and-white shirt.

"Can you see Fast Gun?" she asked her mom. "How's he doing?"

"I'm not sure." Ashleigh frowned worriedly, but when she saw Will looking at her, she quickly added, "But Melanie can handle him."

Ashleigh smiled, but Christina had heard the tightness in her mother's voice. When everybody began talking once more, Christina pulled Ian aside. "Mom seems worried about Fast Gun. What's going on?"

"You know Dani's had the flu the last couple of days," Ian explained in a low voice. "She's his favorite, and Fast Gun's been getting jumpier and jumpier. I checked on him before he went to the paddock, but you know how he hates men. Kevin said he reared and struck at him when he tried to tack him up, so now Maureen's handling him alone."

"Maureen should have said something," Christina said. "I would have stayed and helped."

"It's all right, Chris," Ian said. "I think everything will be okay once Fast Gun starts running."

"There's my girl!" Will announced proudly. He was watching the parade of horses with binoculars. Christina borrowed her dad's. When she got Melanie in her sight, her heart flip-flopped.

Fast Gun was fighting the pony rider. His neck was frothy with sweat, and his eyes rolled wildly. Melanie was stroking his neck with one hand, trying to soothe him, but the colt seemed oblivious to her.

Christina glanced at Will, telling everybody within hearing distance that Melanie was his daughter. Melanie hadn't had any mishaps on the track since she'd started racing, and Christina hoped her cousin's good luck would hold out.

Christina kept her fingers crossed until Fast Gun was loaded in the starting gate. The colt snaked his head sideways, trying to bite the assistant starter. Perched on the huge animal, Melanie seemed tiny and helpless to do anything. Finally the starter took hold of Fast Gun's ear, which made the colt stand still, but Christina bet it was also making him mad.

Christina kept the binoculars aimed on Melanie. Beside her, she could hear Will and Susan chattering with nervous excitement. Fortunately, they didn't have a clue how nutty Fast Gun was acting.

Christina's own stomach fluttered. *You can do it, Mel*, she urged silently.

"It's post time!" rang through the grandstand, and seconds later the starter's gun sounded and the gates flew open.

Christina tensed when she realized that the assistant starter had held on to Fast Gun's ear an instant too long. The colt broke late. When he leaped from the gate, his ears were pinned and his gait was rough.

Melanie tried to pull him together, but the colt must

have grabbed the bit in his teeth, because he rushed headlong down the track, plunging into the middle of the field of horses. As they rounded the first bend Christina couldn't see Melanie's face, but she could tell by her body language that she was fighting the colt, trying to get him under control. Fast Gun wasn't responding.

He charged into the flank of Nevermore, the lead horse. Suddenly Fast Gun's right foreleg hooked Nevermore's left heel. Fast Gun tripped, went down on his knees, and skidded in the soft dirt. Melanie flew over the colt's head, landing on her stomach. Jumping to his feet, Fast Gun leaped over Melanie and, riderless, continued to run the race.

Christina screamed as the rest of the horses in the field came thundering toward Melanie. *They were going to run right over her!*

13

At the last second Melanie rolled into a tight ball and covered her head with her hands. Two jockeys managed to steer around her. The third couldn't get clear in time. His horse went right over Melanie, his hoof knocking into her back.

Christina clapped a hand to her mouth, stifling another scream. She could hear her mother gasp and someone moan. When she glanced at Will, his face was stark white.

Christina forced herself to look back at the track. Already several officials were running out. Melanie was kneeling, and when an official reached her, he helped her to her feet. By that time, someone from the emergency crew had arrived. Melanie shook her head at him, then raised her hand and waved at the crowd in the grandstand.

Christina exhaled with relief. She was all right!

"She's okay," Christina said to everyone, giddy with relief.

Susan was crying, and Will was patting her back to comfort her. Ashleigh and Mike both had stricken expressions on their faces.

Christina turned back to watch the race's finish. Fast Gun was still galloping with the other horses, crossing the finish line in third place. When an outrider cantered up to get him, the colt ducked away. Tail streaming, he pranced down the track as if he'd won the race.

"Thank goodness he's okay, too," Christina told Ms. McFarland, who was staring straight ahead, a numb expression on her face.

Ms. McFarland turned to Mike and Ashleigh. "I think it's time to take your advice," she told them. "As soon as Fast Gun recovers from the race, call the vet and have him gelded."

"Good idea," Mike said soberly.

"You okay?" Parker said, squeezing Christina's hand.

She nodded. "I just hope Melanie's not hurt. Let's go down to the jockey room. I know they won't let us in, but at least she'll know we're waiting for her."

When she told her mother their plan, Ashleigh nodded in agreement. "We have to run over to the Sky Theater so we don't lose our table for dinner. We'll meet you there, all right?"

Christina and Parker hurried down to the jockey room. Since the last race was over, the jockeys who had ridden for the day were leaving. Christina spotted George, dressed in jeans and a button-down dress shirt.

Christina's heart was still thumping from Melanie's fall, but now was as good a time as any to settle things with George. Melanie's accident had reminded her how dangerous racing was without having a jockey causing problems. "Excuse me a minute, Parker," she said.

"You want me to go with you?" he asked when he saw whom she was looking at.

"No, it's all right. Just keep an eye out for Melanie."

Christina hurried to catch up with the jockey. "George?" she called, trying to keep her voice from quavering. Stopping, he turned to see who had said his name. "I'd like to talk to you."

When he saw it was Christina, George frowned with disgust and continued on his way. She jogged up beside him. "Please?"

He halted. "You've got two seconds. My youngest boy's having a birthday party tonight. I don't want to miss it."

So he is *human*, Christina thought. She hesitated, not sure what to say. She couldn't apologize, because noth ing had ever been her fault. She couldn't threaten him, because that wasn't her style. So how was she going to reach him?

"How old is Robby going to be?" she asked.

He cocked one brow. "How do you know his name?"

"Because his picture is hanging on the notice board, and I've heard you talk about him."

"Oh." His expression softened. "He'll be three."

"That's nice."

"Right." George crossed his arms over his chest and eyed Christina suspiciously. "Your two seconds are up."

Christina swallowed hard and her palms started sweating. "I just wanted to say," she began, trying to keep her voice steady, "that you've proved your point. You've shown me that I'm an inexperienced bug who can easily get squashed. I've got my suspension and I think we're even. From now on I hope you'll leave me alone, so we can just go out there and ride our best."

He studied her for a minute, then shrugged. "Okay."

"Okay?" *That's it?*

"That's what I said." And without another word, he left.

Parker bounded up. "What happened? Why'd he run off? Did you threaten him with tacks under his saddle?"

161

Christina let out her breath, then shook her head. "Not exactly. Look, there's Melanie."

Her cousin was the last to leave. She'd changed into a miniskirt, silky tank top, and platform sandals. When she came through the door, she was limping slightly, but when she saw Christina and Parker, she put a smile on her face and hurried over. "Hey, guys, did you catch my award-winning performance?" she quipped.

"We sure did! You gave your dad some more gray hairs—and totally scared me," Christina said, giving her cousin a hug. Melanie tried to hide her wince of pain, but Christina caught it anyway. Her cousin *wasn't* okay. Christina pulled back to ask Melanie what was going on, but Kevin came hurrying up, looking frightened.

"Are you all right?" he asked Melanie.

"It was nothing," Melanie scoffed. "I wasn't even scared." She gave Christina a worried look. "Did my dad really freak out?"

Christina nodded. "He and Susan were pretty shaken. Susan was crying. I tried to reassure him that you were all right."

"Man, why did I have to fall when my dad's here?" Melanie moaned. Christina sympathized. Will had been upset enough by the thought of Melanie racing. The accident wasn't going to help.

"Well, I guess we should head over to the grandstand. I have to face him sometime," Melanie said, putting on a brave expression.

"How's Fast Gun?" Parker asked Kevin as the foursome started walking back toward the grandstand.

"Mean. When I took off the saddle, he tried to eat me."

"Ms. McFarland said she's finally going to geld him," Christina said. As they went up to the Sky Theater, the restaurant on top of the grandstand, Christina noticed Melanie biting her lip nervously. Her cousin had put on blusher, but her face was still pale. Christina could tell Melanie was hiding something. Was she hurt, Christina wondered, and just not admitting it to anyone? Or was she simply worried about her father? Either way, Christina knew she should keep an eye on her.

When no one was looking, she gave Melanie's hand a squeeze. "Your dad will understand," she whispered. "It'll be okay." She only hoped she was right.

"Mel?" Christina knocked on her cousin's bedroom door. "Are you asleep?" When she didn't hear anything, she opened the door. The room was dark, and Melanie was sprawled facedown on the bed.

Christina had worried about her cousin the whole evening. All through dinner Melanie had laughed cheerfully and loudly, telling everyone within earshot

163

how the accident hadn't rattled her at all. But when the two girls had gone to the rest room, she'd seen Melanie hide another wince of pain. Something was going on, though Melanie had refused to talk about it right then. Fortunately, Will had had the good sense not to confront his daughter in front of guests, but he and Susan had requested that Melanie drive home with them.

Her cousin had gone straight upstairs when they'd arrived home, but Christina knew that Melanie and her dad must have talked about the race.

"Mel?" Christina whispered. Holding her breath, she listened, but Melanie didn't respond. *She's probably wiped out from the fall,* Christina figured. She was shutting the door when she heard a muffled sob.

Opening it, she crossed to Melanie's bed and sat on the edge of the mattress. "That bad, huh?" she asked, referring to Will's reaction.

"Actually, my dad was pretty decent. Especially when I reminded him about the summer he went kayaking and almost drowned, and the winter he went extreme skiing and was buried by an avalanche."

"Then what's wrong?" Christina could just make out Melanie's tear-stained cheek.

"Me! That's what's wrong. I hurt *everywhere*. Even my teeth hurt." Rolling over, she sat up, the covers draped over her knees. "Look." Reaching around, Melanie lifted the hem of her T-shirt. Christina gasped.

In the middle of her cousin's back was a dark blue bruise the size of a softball.

"That's horrible! Why didn't you say something?"

Melanie dropped her T-shirt. "I couldn't. Everybody thinks I'm invincible."

"But that must hurt like crazy. Tomorrow you'd better go to the hospital and get it looked at."

"No way. Nothing's broken. And I don't want Dad to see it. He'd send me to sewing camp for the rest of the summer." She leaned back against her pillow, dark circles under her eyes. "It'll be all healed in a few days."

"Anything I can do?"

"Don't tell *anyone*. Okay?"

"Okay."

The two girls were silent for a minute. Christina was glad that Melanie had confided in her. It was hard to keep a secret all to yourself. Still, when she glanced at her cousin, she could tell something else was wrong.

"Are you going to tell me what else is bugging you?"

Melanie ran her fingers through her cropped hair. "I lied to you when I said I wasn't scared. I was *petrified*." Tears began to roll down her cheeks. "I've seen replays of jockeys falling in the middle of a race and getting— and getting—" She was unable to say the words. "I was so lucky that no one was hurt. And the thing is, the accident was my fault."

"How do you figure it was your fault? Fast Gun was nutso."

"But I was too cocky. I figured I could handle him. I didn't take Maureen's advice. She told me what to do to keep him under control. Only I didn't listen. I thought I knew what was best. And I blew it. He got away from me from the get-go."

Pulling a tissue from the box on Melanie's bedside table, Christina handed it to her cousin. Melanie blew her nose nosily.

"Monday I'm going to apologize to Maureen," Melanie continued, letting out a sigh. "You know, in a way I'm glad I fell. I was getting too confident. From now on, I won't be such a know-it-all. I'll listen to advice and maybe even be more careful. *Maybe*," she added with a wry laugh.

"But you'll still be known as Mighty Mel, the winningest at Whitebrook. Okay?" When Melanie didn't look too sure, Christina added, "Hey, everyone has bad days. Look at me, the queen of bad days." Christina's shoulders slumped as she remembered her suspension.

Why had everything gone so wrong all of a sudden?

"Isn't there some way to convince the stewards to let you ride sooner?" Melanie asked. "You were doing so great!"

"I don't think so, Mel." Christina could feel the tears welling up in her eyes. "This time I really blew it."

"What a workout!" Ashleigh called cheerfully Tuesday morning. Christina had just finished galloping Star on Whitebrook's track, and her cheeks glowed from the sheer thrill of riding him.

"Thanks!" Christina called as she trotted past. Ashleigh had just driven up to the barn. "Where'd you go so early this morning?"

Slowing Star, Christina walked him in a circle to cool him down. Since it was late morning, the other riders and horses were finished. Christina had kept Star for last so she could take her time with him.

Smiling, Ashleigh propped one foot on the lower fence board. "Oh, I was on a little mission," she said, sounding secretive.

"A mission? Did you look at a new horse or something?" Halting Star, Christina bent over and felt his chest. She was amazed how cool the colt was after his workouts. "You know, Mom, I think you and Star need to race a mile next weekend. Ian and I discussed it yesterday after his workout. Six furlongs is too short. He's just barely getting started. What do you think?"

"I've been thinking the same thing. In fact, Ellis Park hosts the Laurel Stakes, which is a mile. It'll be the perfect race. I'm going to have Mike scratch Star from the Magnolia Stakes and enter you and Star in the Laurel.

With Brad's permission, of course."

Christina straightened. Flinging one leg over the pommel, she slid to the ground, then turned to loosen the girth. "You mean *you* and Star," she corrected.

Ashleigh grinned. "No, you heard me right the first time."

Swinging around, Christina faced her mother. "What are you talking about?" she demanded.

"I talked to the stewards this morning. They shortened your suspension to seven days. You'll be eligible to ride Star in his next race."

Christina's mouth fell open in complete astonishment. Butterflies of excitement began to flutter about in her stomach. "Yes!" She spun around and flung her arms around Star's neck. "Did you hear that, boy?"

Star bobbed his head and snorted loudly. Suddenly it dawned on Christina what her mother had done. "But you said you wouldn't talk to the stewards!" she accused, staring at her mother.

Ashleigh shrugged and kicked at a pebble before leveling her gaze at Christina. "You mean I behaved just like you did when you rode claimers for Phil Oberman *before* you even asked for permission?"

Christina's face turned bright red. "How'd you find out about that?"

"Phil mentioned something about a race you had the week before you talked to us about it. And it wasn't hard to find out there was never any clinic at Edge-wood."

Totally ashamed, Christina dropped her eyes. "Sorry. I know it was wrong. But I couldn't think of any other way to get more races in."

"I understand," Ashleigh said. "Which is why I never said anything. And all the more reason for you to understand why I went behind your back. Chris, you and Star belong together," she continued. "I want you to be his jockey for his next race. Talking to the stewards was the only way for that to happen."

Christina peered up at her mom from under the brim of her helmet. "You're not going to ground me for riding claimers behind your back?" she asked, fidgeting with the reins.

"Let's just say we're even." Ashleigh shook her head. "But no more sneaking around, or next time I won't be so understanding. Promise?"

"Promise." Christina smiled at her mother, happiness and relief filling her at the same time. "So what did you say to the stewards to get them to change their minds? I mean, I hope you didn't get George in trouble, or I'll never be able to show my face in the jockey room again."

Ashleigh's eyes twinkled. "The Townsends have given lots of money over the years to all of the Kentucky tracks. When I mentioned that Brad Townsend wants to

169

see you up on Star in the Laurel Stakes, the stewards admitted that they'd been a little harsh on you."

"Brad wants me to ride Star?" Christina demanded, amazed.

"Well, Parker and I are still working on him," Ashleigh admitted. "But he doesn't have any choice—you're Star's jockey."

14

"Ms. Griffen," a reporter called when Christina came out of the jockey room dressed in her blue-and-white silks, "do you think you and Wonder's Star will have a better race today than you two had last month?"

"It's Ms. Reese," Christina said, and pointed at the pad in the reporter's hand as if to make sure she made note of the correct name. "Christina Reese. And yes, I think Wonder's Star is going to *rule* the Laurel Stakes."

The reporter grinned. "May I quote you?" she asked.

Christina laughed. "Star is built and bred for distance. Even though he's a two-year-old, we think a mile race will be perfect for him. We'll see—*anything* can happen."

Anything, she repeated silently, reminding herself that only a couple of days before, she hadn't even thought she would be riding Star in this race.

The woman scribbled on her pad. "You sound as if you know this colt well," she commented.

"I've been pretty involved in his training ever since he was a foal," Christina said, smiling at her understatement.

"That's kind of unusual in this business."

A smile spread over Christina's face. "Oh, Star and I aren't that unusual. I can think of at least one other horse-and-jockey team who had a similar relationship."

The reporter must have noticed Christina's proud smile. "You mean your mother, Ashleigh Griffen, and her horse Wonder—Star's dam, am I right?"

"Right," Christina said. "Now if you'll excuse me, I've got a horse to ride!"

Hurrying to the paddock, Christina searched for Star. She saw him immediately, his proud stance and glistening copper coat standing out among the other horses. When she saw who was leading him, she stopped in surprise. "Parker?"

"At your service, madam." Parker bowed at the waist. "You were there for me and Sterling at my event. Now I want to be here for you and Star." Stepping back, Parker gestured toward the colt as if he were presenting him at a fashion show.

Christina ran her hand down the colt's gleaming neck. "Wow, he looks great. You make a terrific groom.

Thanks." Standing on tiptoe, she kissed Parker softly on the cheek. "For everything."

When a couple of the other grooms and jockeys whistled and made catcalls, Parker blushed. "Well, it wasn't totally my idea," he admitted as he led Star to the saddling stall. "Your mom and dad decided to watch the race from the grandstand with my parents. They're all pretty excited."

"I hope I don't disappoint them." Looking around, Christina hunted to see if her parents had come down to the paddock first. She spotted them along the rail. Her father gave her a thumbs-up sign. Ashleigh waved and called, "We'll be watching! Good luck!"

Christina smiled. She knew her parents would be there for her no matter what happened. "I should say I hope I won't disappoint *your* mom and dad."

Parker squeezed her hand. "You won't. You *can* do it, Christina. And as far as Star goes"—Parker scratched under the colt's forelock—"we know he's got what it takes. Come on. Let's saddle up!" Parker grabbed the blue-and-white blanket.

As Christina helped Parker saddle Star, she gnawed her lip, worrying about the race. Star had drawn the number five slot, which wasn't such a hot place to be in the field of eight colts. And that morning she'd found out George was riding a colt named Now or Never. Not a good omen, she figured. Though none of the jockeys had razzed her in the jockey room, she still felt the tension. The Laurel Stakes had the biggest purse of the day. Every jockey wanted to win.

"Hungry?" Parker asked as he came around Star's rump.

"Huh?"

Parker touched her bottom lip. "The way you're chewing on your lip, I thought maybe you didn't have breakfast."

"I'm just worried."

Parker grinned. "A little worry never hurt anyone," he reminded her. "Gets your adrenaline pumping. Ready?"

Christina took a deep breath. This was it. This was the race she'd been preparing for. "Ready."

Parker gave her a leg up. Once she was sitting on Star, Christina felt better—as if she were on top of the world. When Parker led them to the paddock gate, a deep voice bellowed, "Go get 'em!"

It was Brad Townsend, standing by the rail. He and Lavinia raised their plastic glasses in salute.

"Thanks!" Christina called back in shock. She glanced down at Parker, who looked just as surprised to see his parents acting so enthusiastic.

Parker shrugged. "Maybe they've had too much champagne," he joked, and Christina giggled.

When they reached the gate, Parker reluctantly

unsnapped the lead from Star's bridle. Reaching up, he touched Christina's hand. "Good luck," he mouthed before stepping back.

As they strode onto the track, Christina's chest felt tight with emotion. She closed her eyes, shutting out the roar of the crowd so that she could concentrate on Star. When he broke into a trot, she felt his powerful muscles flowing beneath her. The sound of his hooves thudding in the soft footing brought back the memory of all the wonderful early morning gallops they'd had in the past.

Opening her eyes, she leaned down and rested her hand on his withers. His coat was warm and soft. His brown eyes looked about with quiet confidence.

"You know you can win, Star," Christina whispered. "And I'll do my best to give you the ride you deserve."

Star broke into an easy canter. Christina could tell by his smooth, balanced stride that he was in peak form. Now it was up to her. She had to pay attention and use all that she'd learned the past month to ride him to victory.

The first four horses loaded quickly, none of them balking at the gate. When it was Star's turn, Christina patted him soothingly. He walked right in and the gate clicked shut behind them.

While Christina waited for the others to load, she glanced down the line of stalls. George and Now or

Never were number seven. Vicky Frontiere was in the third stall on Heads Up. Right next to her was Raoul Menendez on Crown Prince, the top-rated colt according to the *Daily Racing Form*. In the fourth stall Jeremy Rush was sitting on Hornet's Nest, the colt who had beaten Star in the Spring Stakes.

Christina swallowed hard. It was going to be a tough race.

But we can do it.

She heard the last stall door slam shut, and when she heard the announcer holler, "It's post time!" she twined her fingers in Star's mane. Her heart was beating so hard, she imagined she could hear it slamming against her chest.

"Ready?" she whispered to Star as she positioned herself low on his neck. Then the gun went off and the gate flew open.

"They're off!"

Star blasted onto the track like a rocket, Christina holding tightly to his mane. The track loomed before them, smooth and clean. Motionless, she crouched on Star's back, her fingers steady but soft on the reins.

Steady, steady, her grip communicated to Star. *We have a mile. Take your time.*

Christina glanced to her right. Heads Up was galloping beside them, Vicky's red-and-green silks as colorful as Christmas. To Christina's far left, Raoul hugged the rail on Crown Prince, with Hornet's Nest on his tail. The rest of the field was strung in a ragged line behind them.

Where was George? Christina shot a quick glance over her shoulder and spotted him riding right up behind Star.

Momentary panic filled Christina, and her fingers tightened on the reins. Instantly Star slowed.

Calm down, she admonished herself. She remembered her mother's words after the disastrous Spring Stakes: "You and Star communicate too well. He reacts to everything you do. When you become confident, you two will be unbeatable."

She had to be confident. The moment had come.

Christina took a deep breath, steadying herself. Her grip softened on the reins. She pressed her fists against Star's neck. "We can do it," she whispered, the words flying from her mouth with the rushing wind.

In a tight pack they headed down the backstretch. They blew past the three-eighths pole, 660 yards from the wire. Christina's pulse quickened as she realized how fast the race was going. She glanced left, then right. Raoul and Jeremy were still battling out ahead of her on the rail; Vicky had pulled ahead on the outside. She and Star were in fourth place. They'd have to go soon if they wanted to move up.

Suddenly George nipped into the hole where Heads

Up had been—right beside Star. Christina's heart flew into her throat, but she caught herself before panic set in.

Forget George. Forget the other horses. It's just you and Star.

They thundered around the final turn, Star's stride strong and even. He was tugging on the reins, telling Christina he wanted to go. The three-sixteenths pole flashed by. If Star had more to give, now was the time.

"Go, Star!" Christina shouted, her hands kneading into his neck. "You can do it!"

The colt burst ahead as if he'd been waiting for this all along.

They flew past Hornet's Nest and Crown Prince and tucked into the rail beside Vicky and Heads Up. Barreling down the homestretch, Christina couldn't hear the roar of the crowd or the cry of the announcer. She didn't feel the wind slapping her cheeks or the sweat rolling down her forehead. There was nothing ahead of them but empty track, and even Heads Up was behind them now.

Christina was only aware of Star and his incredible power as his hooves tore at the track, his muscles surging beneath her as he raced toward the finish line.

And when they charged past the wire, leaving the others far behind, Christina knew that Star had wanted this win as much as she.

"And Wonder's Star wins the Laurel Stakes by four

lengths!" the announcer cried out. "A colt to watch out for, especially since he's Ashleigh's Wonder's colt."

Christina stood in the saddle, one fist raised triumphantly in the air as they swept past the roaring grandstand. As Star slowed to an easy canter Christina reached down to rub his glistening neck. They passed a group of reporters on the rail, and the cameras clicked and flashed.

Christina didn't have to see the headlines to know what they would say: "Wonder's Star and Christina Reese—the Perfect Team!"

Alice Leonhardt has been horse-crazy since she was five years old. Her first pony was a pinto named Ted. When she got older, she joined Pony Club and rode in shows and rallies. Now she just rides her Quarter Horse, April, for fun. The author of more than thirty books for children, she still finds time to take care of two horses, two cats, two dogs, and two children, as well as teach at a community college.

THOROUGHBRED

If you enjoyed this book, then you'll love reading all the books in the THOROUGHBRED series!

At bookstores everywhere,
or call 1-800-331-3761 to order.

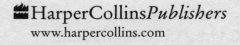HarperCollins*Publishers*
www.harpercollins.com

THOROUGHBRED

**All books are
$4.50 U.S./$5.50 Canadian**